Nihad S'rees was born in Aleppo, Syria in 1950. After training and working as an engineer, he became an acclaimed novelist, playwright and screenwriter. After finding himself under increasing surveillance and pressure from the S government, in 2012 he left for Egypt and now lives and works in exile.

Max Weiss is a faculty member at Princeton University, specializing in the culture and history of the Middle East, and an award-winning translator of contemporary Arabic literature.

NIHAD SIREES

THE SILENCE
AND
THE ROAR

Translated from the Arabic by
Max Weiss

PUSHKIN PRESS
LONDON

Pushkin Press
71–75 Shelton Street, London WC2H 9JQ

Original title: *Al Samt Wal Sakhab*
© Dar al-Adab, Beirut, 2004
French translation: Editions Robert Laffont, S.A., Paris, 2012

English language translation © 2013 Max Weiss

This edition first published by Pushkin Press in 2013

ISBN 978 1 908968 29 6

Set in 11 on 14.5 Monotype Baskerville
by Tetragon, London
and Printed and bound in Great Britain by
CPI Group (UK) Ltd, Croydon, CR0 4YY
www.pushkinpress.com

THE SILENCE
AND THE ROAR

CHAPTER ONE

I T WAS INTENSELY HOT. I could feel that the sheet underneath me was completely soaked through without even opening my eyes. I was having trouble breathing it was so hot, as sweat accumulated in pools that would trickle down my neck. I wiped the spot just above my lip where I was accustomed to finding sweat collected in thin little rivulets. I rolled over onto my left side to look up at the clock hanging above the window; dazzling light streaming in made it impossible to see its hands. It turned out to be eight thirty, though the hubbub in the street made it seem as though the day was already half gone.

I peeled off my sopping wet undershirt and sighed, a sigh that betrayed my irritation at having to go out and buy a fan. I was annoyed at myself because I had already asked my mother for money several times, but instead of actually buying the fan I would always spend it all on food and tobacco. I preferred to stay in bed, refreshing myself by pouring a bottle of water over my head and bare chest. This was a trick Lama taught me. She would also moisten a towel and press it against my naked body until I cooled down. Then, with two fingers, she'd slide it across my chest, passing through my midsection and all the way down to my feet. Until the water soaking the towel warmed up I felt an invigorating coolness, at which point either I got hard and Lama would respond, or else I played dumb and pretended not to know what she was up to with this towel game, which would only make her succumb to pampering me even more.

Barely eight thirty in the morning and the sounds outside were all chaos. Sounds turned into noise as a bullhorn amplified a goddamned voice reciting inspirational poetry, utter gibberish that was only interrupted by the occasional barked instruction. The meaning of all those words got lost because another loudspeaker was simultaneously blaring motivational anthems. Meanwhile schoolchildren parroted the refrain, "Long live... Long live…"

Why didn't I get some kind of a curtain to shade my eyes from the blinding daylight instead of taping white paper against the glass? My mother had told me on more than one occasion that she was willing to sew one for me; all I had to do was take the measurements of the window. I promised to do so just as soon as I could get my hands on a measuring tape, but I couldn't find a single person who had one of those contraptions that reels the tape back up with a spring mechanism as soon as the measurement has been taken. My mother suggested that I could even measure the window with a long thread but I never did that either.

One of these days I'll just lug the wardrobe over and use it to block the window so I can get some relief from the noise and light.

Lama's flat is warmer than mine because its only window faces south. She has a bigger bed that doesn't squeak the way mine does. Her bathroom is adjacent to the kitchen, that is, at the opposite end of the two-room flat. One room for sleeping (the one with the window), the other for living, and a spacious hallway connecting the two that leads to the bedroom at one end and the kitchen and the bathroom at the other. My flat has three rooms: one where I sleep, another where I work and a third where I entertain my friends when they come over. Each room has a window and the kitchen has a door leading out onto a small balcony. My flat gets a lot of light and has good airflow; still, whenever I am here I'm always hot and incessantly sweating. I wake up drenched in my own sweat. Light and street noise and the loudspeakers all flood the flat because my building overlooks two streets with a number of mosques, a government building and a school. Whenever I complained to my mother about the heat and the noise, she would tell me my flat is in an "articulate" neighbourhood. I never quite understood why she would describe a neighbourhood as articulate! I think what she meant to say is that it's a desirable neighbourhood, that it gets a lot of foot traffic and that it's located at the junction of several main thoroughfares. Our neighbourhood is not articulate, though. No, it's just loud because of the tremendous amount of noise that fills it up, piercing it, piercing my eardrums, obliterating my calm. Not only is Lama's flat quieter, it's also more serene. She can barely hear the sounds of her neighbours' footsteps. The sounds of cars and muezzins don't travel very far inside and none of the building's residents has any children. Her bed doesn't even squeak. What a luxury! Here when I shut the windows in order to block out the noise, I end up roasting in an infernal desert summer.

I wished Lama were with me so that I could ask her to moisten the towel, hold it between her thumb and forefinger, and slide it over my naked body, but she wasn't; she was in her own private oven. Whenever I slept at her flat she was amazed at how sweaty I got. Imagine her going to the bathroom every once in a while, getting in the shower and then coming back without drying off. She would rub herself against me in order to cool me off and then start sobbing because I was too hot to do anything, least of all to be caressed in that hellish climate. I would always get dressed and slip out before dawn.

I got up at five minutes to nine. The din quieted down for no apparent reason. I believe that people are more sensitive to noise while they're horizontal, so I make a point of getting out of bed immediately upon waking. As soon as I get up I focus on household matters. I see the chaos: my clothes strewn all over the floor, on the bed, the chair. I stare at myself in the mirror. I close the bathroom door behind me and the noise recedes. The bathroom is the least noisy place in my flat because it resembles a sealed box. Whenever the noise becomes unbearable I seek refuge in the bathroom. At Lama's flat I strain to hear the sound of someone else's breathing; in mine I can't even hear the sound of my own.

In the bathroom I took stock of what I did yesterday. For some time I have been suffering from unhappiness and self-loathing because I don't actually do much of anything. Yesterday was like the day before and like the day before that and like any day months earlier. I don't do anything any more. I don't write. I don't read. I don't even think. I lost the pleasure of doing things some time ago. And so while I'm in the bathroom today my mood gets even worse for not having done anything yesterday. In the past I used to make sure to do something in order to reap the pleasure of achievement the following morning. The pleasure of doing something leads to the pleasure of accomplishment. Pleasure begets pleasure and all that good stuff. A kind of cascade is initiated through the simple act of doing. But I have no idea how to empower that act because I lost the fuel for it somewhere, sometime, and I don't know how to get it back. I haven't found the right occasion to get it back. Action is something of the past while the present has become a continuous state of unhappiness or self-loathing that I suffer as soon as I set foot inside the bathroom. If it were up to me I would stay in bed and spare myself this daily accounting but the noise coming from outside forces me to get up.

Noise. Derived from the foul verb *to make noise*. I haven't come across another verb in the Arabic language that is quite so foul. I prefer the word roar. In my story I will use the two words interchangeably, so I should explain myself more precisely by getting a little more intimate and recounting a dream I once had. I am up on stage wearing a black suit and a wine-coloured tie. String musicians take their seats and begin tuning their instruments. The orchestra conductor hasn't arrived yet and the sounds of tuning grow steadily louder. The instruments produce their sounds all at once, without any harmonization or arrangement keeping them together. Loud, ghastly noise is emanating from these musical instruments that, upon the orders of the conductor, will soon play the most beautiful melodies in unison. But the

11

conductor never shows up and the noise just goes on and on, without rests or intermission. Melody is sound; tuning is noise. I try to block my ears with both hands until my head nearly caves in. I continue dreaming of noise throughout the night. When I finally wake up my ears hurt, my head is heavy and my room drowns in street noise.

Without shaving I left the bathroom and went into the kitchen. I drank a glass of cold milk and spooned some jam right out of the jar. I gazed out at the building across from mine. Veiled women on their balconies or at their windows were looking down at the street in silence. There wasn't a single woman or child who had not come out to gawk lazily. I cautiously approached the balcony door and when it opened the fury of the roar caught me by surprise. I wasn't dressed yet. I was still in my underpants. Wrapping myself up in the balcony curtain with one hand and holding the empty glass of milk in the other, I stepped outside. Looking down at our corner where the two streets intersect, I saw a remarkable scene. Both streets were packed with crowds that undulated and surged as hundreds of pictures of the Leader fluttered over the heads of the masses like waves on the sea.

I got dressed and left the building. I wanted to escape the heat and the noise by going outside but it was the same hell out there.

When I reached the bottom of the stairs, the entire scene was visible before me. Because the converging hordes had blocked the entrance, that was where the shouting was at its most intense, seeping into the entryway and echoing louder because of the hollowed-out space inside the walls and the ceiling. I stood on the first step wondering how I would ever be able to shove my way through and out into the street, past those noisy throngs of people organized into rows that surged forward. In fact, I was seized by the sudden fear that grips a swimmer who has just come face to face with a giant shark.

Some young men carrying portraits of the Leader congregated in the entryway and lit cigarettes, leaning against the cool walls and exhaling smoke out of their filthy mouths. Apparently they had left the hordes in order to relax in the shade and cool off a bit. They stared at me derisively, as if there was something funny about the way I stood there on the first step. As I stepped down and got closer to them, other people lost their balance and surged inside like a human torrent from the tremendous pressure of the crowd outside, causing some to fall down on the ground and knocking me forward. This spectacle captured the young men's attention so they forgot about me, making fun of the others instead. A few seconds later two of the organizers, dressed in khaki with red insignias on their shoulders, pushed their way through and started shoving people back outside the entryway. The young men stood up straight, which made the work of the organizers easier, as they seized them and started forcing them back outside as well.

This was all happening just a step away. An organizer stared at me with bloodshot eyes and just as he reached out to shove me along in front of him I held out my arms to stop him. He mistook me for one of those who had tried to sneak away from the march. He didn't try to stretch out his arms any farther but he didn't pull them back either; he just stood there, frozen, and even though he hadn't asked for clarification, I detected the inquisitive look on his face.

"This is my home."

"You live here?"

"Yes."

"So why aren't you participating in the march?"

"I'm not a government employee and I don't belong to a union. I'm a writer. Fathi Sheen."

This piece of information seemed to make him even more hostile.

"Identification," he demanded fiercely. I showed him my ID and he looked it over. His comrade finished expelling everyone from the entryway and then walked over. He took my ID and read my personal information in silence.

"Fucking cunt traitor," the first one said with the same ferocity.

I thanked him. The second one handed back my ID and looked at me the way one might look at rubbish. Then they both turned round and stormed off, roughly pushing their way through the hordes in order to get out. I swallowed the insult and just stood there, calm and silent. I could no longer bear the swelling noise so I moved closer to the bellowing horde that had been shaped into rows. As soon as I took one step outside, the crowd pulled me along, whisking me far away from the entrance to my building.

After two hundred metres the pavement became less crowded. I stopped outside a chemist to watch the crowd. The chemist's awning shielded me from the sun and a breeze started blowing that dried my sweat. It was a decent spot, one that allowed me to monitor one person who was particularly raucous. In spite of his weight this Comrade was being carried on someone else's shoulders as he chanted, towards what must have been nearly a hundred and fifty people, clapping at them while they repeated whatever he had just chanted. I noticed how badly he had been scorched by the blazing sun. Sweat coated his reddened face, the veins in his neck were bulging and taut, his mouth wide open. He shouted slogans; he didn't just recite them, shouting in a booming voice that shot forth from his iron throat that seemed to have been created for this very purpose.

Some people are born to belong to the ruling party, which loves organizing marches such as this one, people whose corporeal abilities are tailor-made to guide the masses. People like him. If I tried shouting like that I would lose my voice after fifteen minutes but this Comrade, who I suspect had been carrying on like this from the very start of the march, still had strength and solidity in his voice. The Comrade who has been bearing him on his shoulders this whole time must have a sturdy body that is capable of carrying a hundred kilograms for a while, relying on his two hands for balance even as he also strains to yell out the chants at the top of his lungs. Straining like this must make his burden even heavier, and if we add on top of that the heat and his suffocating position, with his head sandwiched between the thick thighs of the man on top of him, and if we add on top of *that* the noise and the clapping and the chants being repeated by a hundred and fifty throats, I do not envy this man who carries a greater load than any bull in the world ever has. All for the Leader.

From a certain angle I could just make out the face of the carrier Comrade. When the procession stopped the chanter was right there in front of me. I felt a kind of lightness watching the carrier's face squashed between the thighs of the chanter on top, and I say that I felt lightness because there wasn't even a small bird pressing down on my shoulders. I was standing on the chemist doorstep, enjoying the shade with my arms folded across my chest. The carrier was chanting, too: should I say I was amazed or found it strange or was surprised? It wasn't enough for him to carry his Comrade in that suffocating position; he thought it incumbent upon him to chant as well. A hundred and fifty throats participating in this convoy isn't enough for the Leader—he needs that one extra throat to chant along. The slogan has a metre and the hundred and fifty people were clapping loudly and jumping up and down as they repeated those slogans that were belted out by the man being carried around. Everyone holding up pictures of the Leader started waving them around as some skipped to the rhythm of the slogan, raising the picture up as high as their arms would go.

Here's an interesting titbit: in my country slogans are arranged into lines of rhyming poetry. I'm sure that the Party has a research institute somewhere dedicated to drafting and crafting slogans according to the particular needs of the era. The masses, our masses, are raised on metred slogans. Every era has a slogan that is repeated nonstop. A few moments earlier I heard a brand new slogan that had been drafted in order to make the people praise God for having created them during the Age of the Leader. The man being carried started off his slogan like this "R… R… Our Leader", and the crowd would repeat after him "R… R… Our Leader". What does that "R" even mean? So long as it rhymed, they would repeat the same line over and over again with ecstatic pleasure. In my country people love rhymed speech and rhymed prose and inspirational metred verse. Just watch how they will repeat phrases that have no meaning whatsoever but that rhyme perfectly well. In the end this means that if the ruler wants the masses to adore him he must immediately set up a centre dedicated to the production of new slogans about him, on the condition that they resemble poetry because we are a people who love poetry so much that we love things that only resemble poetry. We might even be satisfied with only occasionally rhyming speech, regardless of its content. Didn't someone say that the era of mass politics is the era of poetry? If so, then the reverse is also true, because poetry is geared towards the masses just like the prose that I am now writing is intended for the individual. This must be why the slogans of the French Revolution weren't composed as poetry, Mirabeau notwithstanding; rather, prose was the mainstay of Jean-Jacques Rousseau. Prose is oriented towards rational minds and individuals whereas poetry directs and is directed towards the masses. It isn't strange that the curtailment of poetry began in the West. Poetry inspires zealotry and melts away individual personality whereas prose moulds the rational mind, individuality and personality. Finally, I would like to point out that my country still lives in the Age of the Masses, which is why metred speech and rhyming verses are a fundamental requirement in our life. My works and prose writings are the imaginations of a traitor and a fucking cunt, as the man in khaki was kind enough to remind me a little while ago.

But let's return to the hundred and fifty people being led by the carrier and the man on top because the march was on the move again as that noisy human mass started pulling away from my resting spot on the chemist steps. A large group of secondary school students approached, all dressed in matching pseudo-military uniforms that we call khaki. They roared even louder than the first group and were led by another man being carried on the shoulders of a volunteer, or perhaps his carrier was an athletic coach, as I'm inclined to believe. The organizer was shouting slogans into a battery-powered hand-held megaphone. They were repeating the same slogans but in a more distinct manner, which might have had something to do with the fact that they were educated students, pronouncing the slogan correctly, without mumbling its words "One, two, three, four, we love the Leader more and more." I would like to describe this roar for you, if that is even possible for me because the megaphone the student leader shouted through was but one of a total of three assorted noisemakers that were blasting my eardrums at that moment. There were two loudspeakers suspended high above us that I had heard from my house, but now one of them was broadcasting inspirational songs while an announcer with a loud and decisive voice that inspires enthusiasm and affection for the Leader in the hearts of the masses was speaking through the second.

That voice addressed the masses—"O citizens, O citizens"—and then proceeded to describe the affection the

18

masses have for the Leader—also known as the Boss—and the affection the Leader has for his people. In his opinion, the masses were merely a small fraction of this world that adores the Leader because there are also trees and birds and clouds and… by God, even the stones and the dirt tremble as the Leader's feet tread upon them. The announcer also declared that the Leader would guide the people to divine victory.

Now I'd like to make a comparison here between the loud speech the announcer made through the megaphone during the march and the sports commentary during football matches that are broadcast on television. Both commentators talk for the sake of talking, just to say something to the audience, to get them riled up to the point of zealotry. Even if the difference between the two may seem substantial, the similarity lies in stirring up the enthusiasm of the masses. While the sportscaster describes what he is actually seeing on the field, our marchcaster describes something that isn't there at all but strives to make the masses believe in it. The sports announcer must take into account the existence of two competing teams while there is only one, perfectly united team present at our marches, a consummate team that must eliminate all traces of individuality in the crowd and turn all those individuals into droplets in a raging human flood. Any hint of individuality is a threat directed at the Leader's supremacy—what else would be the point of bringing together those crowds if not the elimination of every trace of individuality? Besides, the formation of these marching torrents of humanity is not merely the aggregation of specks in order to make them flow in a particular direction; no, the megaphone announcer is rather meant to help bring together the psychological and intellectual flow of the crowd. When he says that human beings and stones and trees all love the Leader, he is addressing every single speck in that crowd; making each and every one of them believe what they are hearing in that moment, without the use of any logic whatsoever; eliminating any judgement in thought or personality or love among the individuals in this human stream; and corralling the raging emotional flood towards the Leader.

The roar produced by the chants and the megaphones eliminates thought. Thought is retribution, a crime, treason against the Leader. And insofar as calm and tranquillity can incite a person to think, it is essential to drag out the masses to these roaring marches every once in a while in order to brainwash them and keep them from committing the crime of thought. What else could be the point of all that noise? Love for the Leader requires no thought; it's axiomatic. And the Leader doesn't ask you to enumerate the reasons driving you to love him so. You must love him for who he is, simply because he is, and any thought given to the reason why might cause you to—God forbid—stop loving him one day because you might find, by chance, for example, that his eyes blink continuously whenever he speaks and that you have disliked that habit ever since you were young, and your love for him may start to diminish, which is, after all, a very grave sin indeed.

Even though I mentioned a reason for these marches, getting the masses out into the streets requires no special occasion. The justifications are always there: the Leader likes marches and can designate any given day for the people to descend into the streets in some particular city so he can sit back and watch it all on TV. This doesn't have to take place on the same day in every city. If the occasion happens to be, as it was in this case, the twentieth anniversary of the Leader's coming to power, the marches must begin a week before the anniversary and end one week afterwards. Every city has to come out on a certain day so the television crews can film the march, air them live and then archive them. Some people say that a copy of the recording is sent to an archive in the Leader's palace so he can watch them in his spare time.

So we were in the season of celebrations for the twentieth anniversary of the Leader coming to power, nothing more. While I stood on the steps outside a chemist, under an awning that protected me from the scorching sunshine, the march went on and the noise climbed to a crescendo as pictures of the Leader were hoisted higher above the heads of the masses.

Off to my left I detected an unusual movement and saw three Comrades in khaki uniforms rushing inside a building, shoving everyone they bumped into out of their way. As soon as they went in some secondary school students came running out. They were frightened and easily managed to melt back into the stream of the masses. Some people stopped to watch what was going on inside the building and I moved in to have a closer look. The glare from the sun blinded me at first. I couldn't make out anything more than the anguished cries of someone being subjected to a violent beating. As I drew closer the scene came into focus.

21

All three men were pummelling one of those students even as he tried to deflect their punches and protect his body. He knew how dearly it would cost him if he tried to defend himself by actually fighting back. The young man collapsed onto the ground and they proceeded to stomp on him with their heavy boots. After a moment, once the film had completely evaporated from his eyes, I found him staring up at me with tortured and beseeching eyes. How can I describe that gaze? He was imploring me to step in and save him because he wasn't sure that his friends or the soldiers were going to do anything. He had already lost a tooth. Blood was gushing out of his mouth, staining his face and his neck, then his clothes and the ground they dragged him across. Unmoved, he continued staring up at me even as he was kicked all over his body.

I had spent twenty years trying not to get involved in affairs involving the Comrades, purposefully avoiding them, but the sight of that young man's beseeching eyes pressed me to do something. Drawing closer, I grabbed the arm of one of the Comrades until he and the other two stopped their stamping. The young man writhed in pain and spat up blood.

"What did this young man do?" I asked the one whose arm I was clutching.

"Who the hell are you?"

"I want to know what he did!"

My big mistake at that moment was to let go of the Comrade's arm. The three of them quickly tried to figure out my rank in order to know how they should treat me. I should have held onto his arm. I should have squeezed harder instead of letting go. They left the young man there flailing around on the ground and surrounded me instead. Trying to correct my mistake I held my ground and didn't back away. One of them asked to see my identification but I ignored him. In my country you have to create as much ambiguity as you can in order to get out of situations such as this one, and if you're bold enough you can even conjure some kind of imaginary rank in order to protect yourself. I tried to surround myself with ambiguity even though it's my custom not to pretend to be something I'm not.

"You better have a convincing explanation for what's going on here."

"You want an explanation?"

"That's right," I said. "I want a convincing explanation."

"He's a traitor, he tried to get out of the march," said the same Comrade, who appeared to be the others' superior. "Is that convincing enough for you?"

"You could have just written him up instead of beating him like this."

"And just who might you be, sir?" the third one interjected. Up until that point they still hadn't been able to crack my riddle. They had been dealing with me cautiously.

"A citizen," I said.

At that moment their uncertainty dissipated and one of them smiled sarcastically. They returned to their natural disposition.

"A citizen?" asked the second, getting ready to pounce on me.

"ID," the boss said, reaching out his hand.

I took out my identification and handed it over. He snatched it from me and then motioned for the other two to join him as he walked away.

"Where are you going?" I asked. "My ID."

"Come on down to the station and pick it up," he said, without turning round.

They left. I was furious at myself for getting mixed up with them but the young man was still there, writhing, bleeding. I crouched down next to him and examined his face. He looked up at me again, this time in gratitude. I tried to pick him up and could tell that he needed an ambulance. Two young men who were part of his group had congregated by the door and now came over, thanked me and then took him away. I received one more look of gratitude before they disappeared. A young woman alerted me that there was blood on my collar but I walked away unconcerned.

I backed into the side streets, fleeing the crowds and the noise. The shops were all shuttered and there were only a few people around who had managed to slip away from the march but they were holding pictures of the Leader in their hands. The next day they would have to return them to the organizers. I wandered aimlessly for a long time because I hadn't decided whether I was going to my mother's or to Lama's yet, bearing in mind that it wouldn't do me any good to go down to the station right away to pick up my ID because the one who took it wouldn't get back there before nightfall. Besides, I hadn't even asked him which station he meant, the Party building or the *mukhabarat* headquarters, and if it was the *mukhabarat*, which branch of the security services? I tried not to get too obsessed with figuring out the answer to that question because all I wanted to do at that moment was run away from everything connected to the march and everything that had just happened.

I decided to go see my mother because her house is on the outskirts of town. Going to Lama's would mean heading back in the direction I had just come from, crossing over to the other side of the city by passing through those crowd-clogged streets, the very thing I had been trying to avoid in the first place.

CHAPTER TWO

M Y FATHER PASSED AWAY five years ago, leaving behind a gentle and beloved fifty-something widow, a son and a daughter. I am that son. My name is Fathi and I turned thirty-one three months ago. Rather than telling you about me, though, this chapter is about my mother Ratiba Hanim and my sister Samira, who is five years younger than me. Because I'm on my way over to her house at this very moment, I may as well tell you all about my mother before you get to meet her.

My father was a young lawyer when he proposed to Ratiba, who had been spoiled rotten by her family. More than five years had gone by since he graduated from university and still he had not managed to find a suitable wife. He was politically combative and a capable lawyer, well known for being simultaneously antagonistic towards the government and the opposition. As a clever lawyer he would come up with bizarre descriptions for his bitterest enemies: the government of monkeys; the government bureaucrats who consume more than they produce; the government that rules through the negation of hearts; the government bureaucrats who walk on all fours; and other descriptions that would make the ministers laugh and outrage them at the same time. Because he was a liberal he used milder language to criticize the members of the opposition: the chivalrous knights in shining armour; the opposition on sale; spit on me but put me in power; the opposition that depends on God; the opposition op-posing in a fashion show; and so forth and so on.

This young lawyer had created enemies all around him because he published articles packed with such characterizations in a local newspaper, most of whose subscribers were businessmen. The abundance of his enemies and the scarcity of his supporters made it difficult for him to get married, despite the fact that my grandmother was constantly on the prowl for a suitable bride for her combative lawyer of a son. Every time she found someone the prospective bride's family would entertain the groom for one day, receive an "intervention" and advice from my father's enemies on both sides, and then quickly distance themselves from him. Before he got bogged down with despair my grandmother came to him with one last candidate for marriage: Ratiba, the spoiled sister of an urban merchant whose father had passed away. In addition to having inherited a respectable amount of money from her late father, she was a very happy woman. Her most distinguishing features were mirthfulness, joviality, cheer and a marked lack of interest in the affairs of this topsy-turvy world—just what the combative bachelor had been looking for. This lawyer, Abd al-Hakim, immediately went to see her brother, introduced himself and informed him about his enemies in the government and in the opposition, hoping to pre-empt their "intervention" this time. That merchant, whom I would later call Uncle Mufid, asked this quarrelsome lawyer, the one who would become my father, to bring him newspaper clippings of his stinging articles. Mufid spent the night reading those pieces that were supposed to elicit his anxiety but the very next day he announced his consent. My uncle wasn't the kind of person who enjoyed quarrelling with politicians. He was serious and rational—unlike his sister who was apt to laugh at anything—and this is what made people find his swift consent so strange. They viewed as even more bizarre the fact that he had stood steadfast against the sort of smear campaign that in our city we call an "intervention". In my father, Uncle Mufid had found a man fit to become a husband to his sister who never stopped laughing, not even in her sleep.

The couple were married and spent their honeymoon in a respectable hotel at a chic summer resort, overlooking a densely forested valley. It was there that my father discovered the amazing talents of his bride. When he first read his combative articles she would laugh a bit but eventually she stopped laughing at them altogether. Soon she found them banal and began coming up with new descriptions of her own for her husband's political adversaries. He found these so valuable that he even started including them in his articles. This wasn't hard work for my mother. She would come up with such descriptions while putting on make-up or remembering an old joke that would nearly cause my father to fall over from laughing so hard. Because it was so simple for her, my father's articles seemed like a game to her and she encouraged him to caricature those politicians rather than criticizing them so antagonistically. And that's just what he did. He became more and more infamous until the lawyers' union consequently proposed several times that he should retire.

Although I was the first fruit of that humorous marriage, I was as serious as my uncle and as quarrelsome as my father. In her lack of interest in anything important and her perpetual proclivity to laugh, my sister was a carbon copy of my mother. Let me explain what I mean by this "lack of interest in anything important". One day, a powerful earthquake jolted the city, causing buildings to shake intensely. The chandelier in the living room where my mother and my sister sat together for years vigorously swayed back and forth. Some valuable *objets* fell off the bookcase and shattered; the TV set nearly fell down too, as pots and pans clattered onto the floor in the kitchen. I hurried out of my room, trying to calm down my mother, my sister and myself, but I soon discovered that I was the only one in the house who was frightened. My mother simply carried on with what she was doing (reknitting a wool sweater for the third time), calmly watching the chandelier swing. The transistor radio was switched on and the announcer interrupted his broadcast in order to report in a panic that an earthquake had rocked the city. My mother noticed the quaver in his voice and burst out laughing. That was how I found her when I rushed into the living room, bolting from my room all yellow in the face as my sister went on with her homework.

But my father's articles didn't last much longer because the Leader, who had been a petty officer in the army, launched his military coup, liquidating all of my father's enemies in the government and the opposition, and became the undisputed

ruler of the country. The first thing the Leader did was shut
down publication of all newspapers, permitting only one or
two to write anything about the regime, on the condition
that they always articulated its viewpoint. Even though the
newspaper that used to run his articles stopped appearing,
my quarrelsome father failed to grasp as fully as he should
have what had just happened in the country. He wrote one
more article in the same combative spirit, incorporating my
mother's caricatured images, only this time about the Leader
himself, sending it to one of the government newspapers
with a clear conscience. My mother had infected him with
the scourge of fearlessness and peace of mind. He didn't
even wait for the article to be published before reading it
aloud to his colleagues and friends who all hung out at the
same coffeehouse; all he got from them were uneasy smiles.
They could sense the danger of such satirical articles that
caricatured the Leader, and they were right to feel that way.
Now the butt of the joke was the Leader himself, not merely
politicians who wore white smoking jackets.

When one editor read the article the blood froze in his
veins and he felt dizzy, so he sent it along to the editor-in-
chief after tacking on the word "Urgent". When the editor-
in-chief read it the blood froze in his veins as well and he
transmitted it up to the Minister, whose blood boiled in his
veins in outrage, and when he finally transmitted it in turn
to one of the *mukhabarat* agencies, my father was called in
for questioning. His interrogation lasted a full six months.
In order to spare him from having to go home and come
right back again, they decided to simply keep him there in
their dungeons. He came out afterwards transformed from

a combative individual into a pathetic shell, banned from trying cases in a court of law for a period of two years. And so, just like that, my father turned from jokiness to gloominess and started practising law in the most serious way possible. Whenever he heard my mother tell a joke and start laughing, he would sigh and mourn the good old days. At work he was always morose and demanded that everyone remain serious.

But if life and its inscrutable politics treated my father with solemn humourlessness until the day that he died, it bid him farewell with the most hilarious farce. We buried him in a brand new cemetery that didn't have any distinguishing signposts yet. On that day moreover he wasn't the only person being buried there. One of the others was a famous dancer who had a lot of friends and admirers. Rounding out the joke that was his life, the gravediggers forgot which of the two graves contained my father and which the dancer. One of the dancer's biggest fans had requested a headstone to be made by the same man who engraved my father's. When that day arrived and he set the two headstones upon the graves, he made a horrible mistake, placing the dancer's headstone on my father's grave and my father's headstone on hers, which meant that whenever we visited the cemetery we would recite the Fatiha over the dancer's grave, even as scores of her fans, friends and former lovers would show up and place flowers and plants on my father's grave, sitting down beside him in order to shed tears for their dearly departed dancer. The mix-up lasted several months, until one morning, early in the feast of Eid al-Fitr, my mother and my sister accompanied me to the cemetery where Samira, who possesses keen powers of observation, sensed the mistake at once. It was all cleared up soon thereafter.

Thank God, my mother was home. Even though I know she rarely goes out in the morning, the prospect of not finding her there and having to go back out and wander the streets frightened me very much. All public transportation was out of service because of the march and I had walked a long way to her house. Umm Muhammad opened the door and greeted me warmly. Umm Muhammad is the housekeeper I found for my mother after my father passed away. She always welcomes me with extreme kindness; recently she has taken to kissing me on the cheek and squeezing me against her breasts in order to express how happy she is that I have come. When my mother is there she keeps her voice down, speaking to me in a whisper; when I come over and find Umm Muhammad alone she won't stop shouting, causing me to take a step back and ask her to say hello to my mother for me when she returns. After dragging me into the kitchen she spoke in a hushed voice. Taking advantage of my presence she lit a cigarette and started smoking. Umm Muhammad loves to smoke almost as much as she loves to complain about her bleak misfortune—my mother doesn't care for either habit so my presence always cheers her up.

"Where's my mother?"

"In the bedroom."

"What's she doing?"

"Putting on make-up and watching TV."

"TV? Don't tell me she's watching the march."

"Yeah, she's watching the march on TV. You know how she loves to watch those marches. She always finds something to laugh at. She called for me a little while ago when they showed your building."

"You're joking. Can I go in and see her?"

"First sit with me for a bit. Fathi, I want to ask you something about my son, Muhammad. You're a big figure and you know a lot of people, *mashallah*."

"What about Muhammad?"

"I want you to get him a job with the city."

"But I don't know anyone with the city."

"That's impossible, Fathi. You're a well-known personality and your pictures are always in the papers. The mayor must have seen your picture more than once."

"Who told you that? Anyway, I'm a pariah these days and nobody will listen to me. It's been a long time since they published my picture." Hoping to comfort her, I quickly added, "Anyway, don't worry. I'll speak with a friend about Muhammad, but I can't promise a job with the city."

She lifted her eyes towards the sky and said, praying for me, "May God provide you with a suitable woman. Go on now, go and see Ratiba Hanim. She has good news I'm sure she's dying to tell you."

I walked away from her, out of the kitchen that was now enveloped in a haze of Umm Muhammad's cigarette smoke. I crossed the small living room and walked down the long hallway lined with bedrooms and bathrooms. My mother's bedroom was at the end of the hall. I could hear the sound of the march being broadcast live on television as I knocked on the door.

My mother was sitting in bed painting her toenails and waiting for the red polish to dry. She was wearing pink cotton pyjamas and her head was covered with colourful plastic hair curlers. She could easily see the TV from where she was sitting. She opened her arms as wide as she could to welcome me without getting up. I hugged and kissed her and then sat down on one of the chairs with a flower-print satin cover that she pointed me towards as she began to blow on her painted toes.

My mother is a fifty-five-year-old widow who loves life as if she were twenty. She loves looking pretty and youthful and cheerful and insists that world affairs don't matter. Why should we care about what's going in the world? The greatest tragedy she has ever known was the death of my father. She was inconsolable and stayed at home for six months (not out of any religious devotion or anything like that), neglecting her appearance; now I find her sitting on her bed, preoccupied with her looks once again. Since I don't like my mother to be preoccupied with anything and because I hated seeing her upset or depressed, I decided to move out and get my own place. As soon as I had revealed my intention to her, she got all excited about the idea and bought me my own flat. So that she wouldn't be alone I hired Umm Muhammad to be with her when she was lonely and to take care of her.

My relationship with my mother is one of a kind. Every day I visit to sit and watch her, like a man who watches a woman and struggles to figure out what she might need, while she focuses on her appearance. I would make no comment on such matters. I may have grown accustomed to offering Samira some commentary from time to time, but

I would never get involved in my mother's business and she wouldn't interfere in mine. One time she asked me if I had intentions of marrying Lama, and I told her that as soon as I was ready I would let her know. From that point she stopped asking me when I was going to get married or why I didn't think much about marriage. Samira would always probe me about this, which is one reason I hated going over to her place; I knew she was always going to ask me why I preferred to remain a bachelor. She thought I could find a wife more beautiful than Lama. To this day I cannot fathom why she would want such a thing for me. Why would a sister want her brother's wife to be more attractive than the woman he actually loves? Samira married a businessman and is content with his profound dim-wittedness. She married a son of her Uncle Mufid's partner after he declared independence from his father by opening up his own shop selling industrial lathing tools. That was one year before my father died. At first she taught him how to take an interest in how he looked, but he stopped her when she went too far in trying to re-educate him. Instead, he started asking her to become more like him. So that the two of them could live in peace she stopped telling him what to do and started emulating him, even his dim-wittedness. Samira is quite intelligent whereas her husband most definitely is not. In order to make their marriage work she sacrificed her intelligence but refused to give up her love of joking and her lack of interest in the world—the two most important reasons for her marriage's success. Her husband adored her jokes. He would laugh so hard he had to hold on to his sides or else fall over onto his back. But the talent of "not giving a shit", which was my mother's expression for taking no interest in anything, helped her to put up with her husband's idiocy. I imagine that in a few years they're going to have a mentally retarded child.

But let me get back to telling you about my mother because I take such exquisite pleasure in doing so. I already mentioned how I have made a habit of visiting her every day. She is the only person whom I can visit to make my anxiety disappear, to forget about all of my cares. I would plop down wherever I found her, whether it was in the living room or her bedroom, and we would banter nonstop as I watched her attend to her cosmetic needs. She got me interested in news about her friends, where they were having coffee and where they were thinking about going on vacation. She would tell me all the gory details of their family life and ask my opinion about feminine matters such as what she should wear when she goes out at night. Whenever she caught my attention flagging, she wouldn't hesitate to make some funny remark that would make me laugh. But today the television was on and she was sitting on the bed. She had her knees pulled up in order to blow on her toenails and from time to time she'd cast a glance up at the box broadcasting the festivities. We were in the middle of a conversation when she pointed towards the march.

"I saw your building a little while ago."

"Yeah, Umm Muhammad told me."

"Umm Muhammad is unpatriotic for not going out to march," she jeered.

"Yeah, that's what they say about the people who fall behind in the marches, too."

"But you weren't out on the balcony when we saw your flat. What a shame. It's been such a long time since you were on TV. I told Umm Muhammad you should have stood out on the balcony in order to salute the masses."

"I'll go home right now and do just that."

We each smiled at the other's joke. I noticed how tightly crammed together the pictures of the Leader were at the march. Everyone in the crowd held aloft a photo and massive cloth banners were unfurled on the buildings. Even the façade of the hotel in the square had been plastered with a colourful painting of the Leader. How had I not noticed the density of those pictures when I was down there in the thick of it? Apparently television captures things more accurately than one can actually see them in real life because it looks in from outside the event.

"Why are they chanting, 'Supreme, Supreme, the Leader is Supreme'?" she asked me.

"Because he's supreme."

"What's that?" she asked, staring back at me in astonishment.

"Because he's supreme, pursuant to the latest regulations." Taking comfort in the fact that I hadn't changed, she blurted out a wisecrack of her own:

"They should be chanting 'Obscene, Obscene, the Leader is Obscene', because he's so obscenely obese."

"The people shouldn't look at the Leader's imperfections."

"Chunkiness isn't an imperfection. The chant would be more realistic that way. And besides, I love overweight men. Unfortunately your father was skinny so I could never find anywhere to tickle him."

"I'm glad my father was thin and passed that skinniness on to me. Do you really wish he had been fat?"

"I wish he had been like the Leader. I think the Leader likes being tickled."

"How would you know such a thing?"

"Whenever he laughs he keeps his arms down at his sides. That's how a person laughs to prevent someone from tickling him."

"You'd better be careful, Mum. A joke about the Leader costs whoever cracks it six months' hard time."

"That was less a joke than a revelation. Are they going to throw me in jail for revealing that the Leader is constantly under threat of being tickled?"

"Any joke or piece of information that harms the prestige and dignity of the Leader will mean summonses and perhaps even criminal prosecution."

"But I love him, just look at his picture. He has a childlike face that women simply adore."

On the television a segment of the march was a forest of pictures: a horizontal shot just one metre above the heads of the masses, where thousands of pictures were affixed to poster boards with wooden clothes pegs.

"Why do you think they're carrying all those pictures?" she asked me.

"Because the citizen doesn't need to see anything but the Leader's face. Wherever he turns he should find a likeness of the Leader."

"Wouldn't one large picture carried by a group of Comrades be enough?"

"In the Leader's opinion, no. The sight of even a single

person not carrying a picture and not chanting his name makes the Leader uneasy. He feels reassured when he sees everyone holding up a picture of him. A million people must carry a million pictures. Now that's reassuring. He believes this is the way the masses show their affection."

The camera zoomed in on a group of young men who were chanting and jumping up and down in a circle. Some shoving and shouting broke out and the overseer of the circle got nervous as, one after another, the young men started moving away from one particular spot in the middle. It turned out that someone had fallen down and the others were alerting one another about it. The shoving was growing more intense as the centre started to move, meaning that whoever had fallen was now being trampled underfoot. When some other people reached his body they fell as well, and a great commotion took place that resulted in ever more forceful shoving until the producer was forced to turn the camera away. My mind was suddenly preoccupied. I imagined that the one who fell down first might be dead, and that if the stumbling and shoving and violence were to continue more than one person could get killed out in that unbearable heat. My mother understood why I was so nervous.

"It's only death on behalf of the Leader," she quipped. "Don't worry, it's a tremendous honour."

"Before coming over here I saw some Comrades mercilessly beating a young man just for trying to get away."

My mother made sure the polish on her nails was dry and came over to sit down on the other chair. I assumed she was unhappy whenever she became this interested in herself. To me this seemed like compensation for something lost that was never coming back. Her narcissism began six months after she became a widow, though, and now she clings to making herself appear younger than she actually is. She would spend many days beautifying herself without leaving the house at all; by the time she had finished her make-up and was satisfied with the way she looked, night would have fallen already so she simply washed it all off and went to bed. By contrast, ever since the shock of her marriage Samira had neglected herself, only ever modestly putting on make-up when she had to leave the house. Often when I went to see her I would find her without even any foundation on her face.

With the television now in a corner where it was difficult for her to see, my mother said, "Thank God I was born a woman. They don't force us to go out for marches."

"They do too make women go out."

"Right, but they can't make unemployed elderly house-wives do it."

"Thank God, you don't care whatsoever about world affairs."

"You mean my 'not giving a shit'?"

"Yeah, 'not giving a shit'," I said.

Sensing my despair, she stopped focusing on the television and asked, "What's happening with you?"

"What? Nothing..."

"You've been like this for a long time now. Why don't you bring me a joke instead of this depressing silence?"

"You know I'm no good at telling jokes."

"Do you need money?"

"If you're offering me some, I won't say no."

"I'll give you some, but will you write something?"

"You know I'm banned from writing for the papers and my books are never approved for publication."

"Write *something...*"

"I'll write a novel, maybe a play. I haven't decided yet."

"Decide soon. You write so beautifully."

"You never read a word I wrote."

"Your father was a big fan of your writing. And people who like you call me the Writer's Mother."

"That was a long time ago."

"Don't be stubborn. I'll buy your work myself. Offer me a new novel and I'll pay you two thousand dollars."

"Is this some kind of a joke?"

"Hardly."

"All right, my next novel will be about you."

She laughed and her fillings became visible. Her teeth had grown a little bit longer. Once again I could sense how unhappy she had become. Umm Muhammad called us and we went into the living room to have coffee. I felt like Mum was nervous; this was the first time in a while I had seen her this way. She got up from her chair and went to stare out the window; I presumed this was because she was nervous about me but she came back to sit down and told me everything was fine. As she passed by, she caressed my hair with a movement that only she knew how to do.

"Fathi," she said, in a calm and serious voice, "I want you to meet someone very important to me."

"Not a problem."

"But I want to explain the situation first."

"All right, what's the situation?"

"The reason why I want you to meet him."

I put down my cup of coffee to make her feel like I was listening to her very carefully. She held onto hers, moving it in closer to her mouth, then farther away. I watched her as she gazed into my eyes.

"He wants your permission so that we can get engaged."

There was no mistake. I had understood completely what she had just said. Still, I asked, "He wants to get engaged… to you… but he wants my permission?"

"That's right. I mean, we're going to get married but because you're my eldest son he wants to meet you and ask for my hand. Do you understand? Your mother is still a young woman, you know, and five years have passed since the death of your late father and there's a man who wants to marry me. That's all clear enough, isn't it?"

"This is just such a surprise, Mum," I said, buying some time to figure out how I felt about it.

"If I was worried about your reaction, I would have made more of an introduction. I would have alerted you first, but I dived right in instead. Think it over if you want, but you must realize I'm still a young woman and that I'm consenting to this marriage, that is, I simply must get married. Should I set up a meeting with him or do you want some time to think about it first?"

I smiled, turned my eyes away and moved to pick up my cup because cups of coffee help us hide what we want kept hidden. I smiled because my mother wanted to get married. She was confused and wanted my approval. I had never seen her so confused before and it became even more apparent how confused she actually was when she asked me if I needed more time to think about it. Who was getting married anyway, her or me? I looked at her and saw her eyes darting back and forth between her cup of coffee and me. In that moment I felt sympathy for her because I love her so very much, and in that moment I loved her even more than ever before. I wanted to say something that might reassure her but the television we had left on in her bedroom started broadcasting a poem that was being recited by the poet himself to the masses stuffed into the city square and his voice distracted me. In a loud voice the poet intoned, "Supreme one of the nation, the Leader of men and..."

"What do you say, Fathi?"

"Who is this guy?"

"I'm even more surprised than you are. He's very well known and I think you know him."

"I know him?"

"I said I think you know him. His name's Mr Ha'el Ali Hassan."

"I know someone by that name."

"That's the one."

The poet continued reciting his poem: "Heap ashes upon them from your fury, O master."

I feel I must explain who this Mr Ha'el is in order for you to imagine my state at that moment. The word dismay is useless because I wasn't dismayed and the word anger is meaningless because I wasn't angry; I wasn't happy or sad or anything like that. Truth be told I didn't feel much of anything because this Mr Ha'el who wanted to marry my mother had not left any impression on me, not because he was unimportant—just the opposite—but because he was exceedingly important and because I considered myself so far removed from his milieu that I simply could not feel anything. It was like hearing about some American billionaire who went bankrupt or some anonymous person who came into a great fortune. I always used to feel like I was far from interested in certain people, including Mr Ha'el Ali Hassan, because they were like destiny or like an addiction indulged by an addict. Let me try and explain what I mean with another example. Say it so happens that the Leader sacks a particular representative from his post and you read about the story in the newspapers but it has no effect on you, so you hurry on to read the next story. It's the same thing when you read that the Leader has hired one of his supporters and made him a powerful representative or promoted him. After twenty years of the Leader's rule this kind of story leaves a person unresponsive. Any news, even when it is about someone who is about to marry my mother—and here he is, an adviser to the Leader—starts to seem like that story you read in the local papers but take no interest in whatsoever.

Once, when the Leader was visiting a backwater town, he was surrounded by a huge number of cadres. The place was throbbing with the masses that were in turn surrounded by the Leader's entourage, which prevented them from getting any closer to him than was absolutely necessary. The Leader's favourite television cameraman was filming every move he made, particularly his right hand as it rose to salute the masses who were overjoyed by this blessed visit to their forgotten town. Just as all of that was proceeding precisely according to plan, something happened that nobody could have anticipated. The Leader stumbled and lost his balance, and he would have toppled over onto the ground if it had not been for someone coincidentally standing right behind him who was able to grab hold of him, an unknown cadre of no real value. I believe he had been a member of the municipal council in that fair town.

That man, Mr Ha'el Ali Hassan, had good fortune. I say good fortune because in his entire life he had never dreamt of receiving so much as a glance or even a smile from the Leader. So how could it be that he should have acquired this exalted honour of saving the Leader from falling and taking a roll in the dirt in front of millions of people, before those who were present and those who sat at home watching this blessed visit on television? The broadcast was interrupted for a couple of minutes and the people did not see what happened during that break thanks to a wise move by the producer (the tape was cut from the moment he stumbled, the section was excised and it was requested that everyone forget all about it as though nothing had happened; it is never mentioned any more and I'm taking a risk now by even bringing it up, may God forbid...). But anyone who was actually there, standing near the Leader instead of busying themselves with the fevered chanting, would have seen this no-name member of the municipal council acting before anyone else (most importantly, the Leader's private guards) and grabbing him under his armpits with a deft movement at just the right moment. The Leader's bum never touched the ground. He held him up confidently and quickly, supporting his body from behind. Once he had made certain that the Leader could stand, he backed a few centimetres away from him without letting go under his arms because with unparalleled intuition he quickly realized that he should be rewarded for his action. The Leader wheeled round to find that the one who had saved him from falling and who had preserved his dignity, his prestige and the elegance of his clothes was not one of his guards or his shadow who followed him wherever he went, stood behind him and leaned whenever he leaned and moved whenever he moved. Rather it was someone with an ordinary peasant face, sharp eyes and unrestrained ambitions of getting closer to him in order to serve him. He was looking for his big break, which had finally arrived. He bowed to the Leader, who had turned red in the face from his stumble, as if to tell him that he was the one who had saved him and that he was now the one asking to be compensated. The Leader extricated himself from the hands of the municipal council member and in that moment the Leader's shadow tried to shove Ha'el away, gesturing to his boss that the man was interfering but the Leader raised his hand to stop him, then tapped on the municipal council member's arm and said, with a grateful smile on his face, "I thank you..."

The television broadcast returned so that the viewers, who are technically every single individual of this nation, could watch the masses saluting the Leader and chanting for him as the weak-hearted swooned from the heat, the dust and the tremendous amount of effort expended in shouting slogans, and could watch the Leader salute the masses with his right hand in return. The Leader was surrounded by bureaucrats, of both high and low rank, in addition to a large number of security guards who had fanned out all over the place. But the viewers, like those surrounding the Leader, were no longer concerned with that municipal council member because his superiors, the security guards, had shoved him farther and farther away, behind row after row around where the Leader stood. Even as Mr Ha'el took up his position in the background his heart beat powerfully and warm as the adrenaline pumping through his blood spiked and his imagination started to drift off into worlds far removed from this celebration. He focused his mind on the image of the Leader smiling at him and saying, "I thank you..."

The event came to an end. The Leader, his escorts, his bodyguards and the television cameras departed in their 120-car convoy, leaving behind a roar and thick dust. The people went back to their homes and their jobs. The municipal council immediately held a meeting to study the effects of the Leader's visit on the town and the anticipated benefits that would accrue from that visit. However, and how amazing this was, all the council members, including the president, started looking at Mr Ha'el in a new light, with some respect but also trepidation. They no longer silenced him or cut him off when he was speaking. The municipal council president stopped interrupting him abruptly and telling him, "Shut up you, what is this bullshit?" Instead, everyone started listening to him with great interest as he enumerated the benefits that were likely to accrue to the town or the personal benefits that some members and the president of the municipal council might acquire. He was not about to let this chance get away from him, so he reminded them several times how the Leader had smiled at him and thanked him "personally".

A few days later a car from the capital arrived. Kicking up thick dust as it sped into town, the car screeched to a halt outside the municipal council building and three men in fine clothes got out. One of them seemed to be in charge and they all scurried inside the building, unaffected by the glares coming from the pathetic guard, Masoud, who smoked, coughed and spat, and then smoked some more. As they barged into the council president's office like holy warriors they kept repeating the name "Mr Ha'el Ali Hassan". But he wasn't there at that moment because unlike all the other representatives he had not been assigned to any particular work that required his presence. The council president dispatched everyone he could find to go and look for him. After several minutes had passed and they still had not found him, the men from the capital could no longer bear staying put in those chairs where the council president had invited them to sit, and so they set off to search for him themselves, their car kicking up more noise and dust until they found him out in the field feeding one of his calves. They seized him and drove him back to his house where they asked him to wash at once and put on a dark suit and a yellow tie. As they guided him, he was powerless to resist. Outside the house he nearly wet his trousers from fear when his wife Aisha and their five small crying children surrounded them. The street was jammed with people whose curiosity had led them there, as Mr Ha'el, representative of that pathetic municipal council, was smashed between two men in the back seat of the car and it set off, leaving behind a cyclone of dirt, flies and hundreds of unanswered questions floating in the dusty air.

Where are they taking Mr Ha'el?—What happened exactly?—Look how his wife Aisha and their small children are crying!—Is it true they're driving him to one of the security branches?—Is it true he pushed the Leader during the blessed visit and nearly knocked him over?—What has he been charged with exactly?—Why don't they have Sheikh Said perform the prayer of guidance?—Is it true they took him to be executed?—Some say Mr Ha'el was part of a conspiracy against the Leader that was uncovered at the last minute, is that true?—Is it true they've started punishing the corrupt, because Mr Ha'el, as everybody know, steals from the municipal council?—Poor Aisha, to be in this situation.

Lots of questions were asked that day in that backwater town but those who asked them did not get any answers. Mr Ha'el did not return to put an end to their perplexity. Instead, a less noisy car from the capital arrived two weeks later and stopped outside Mr Ha'el's house. Two men got out and ordered Aisha and her children to get ready quickly and come with them. All over again the people were confused about the fate of the father, mother and children; some of them grew even more confused when they saw Mr Ha'el on TV in fine condition, noting that he even smiled affectionately. So what had happened to him after all?

The Leader, along with all the bosses of his security apparatus and his bodyguards, had watched the video of his stumble in that backwater town in order to learn exactly what had happened. Why had he slipped? Why wasn't his shadow behind him at that moment? And scores of other questions that the Leader was careful to ask his assistants after any emergency. The bosses were sitting upright on both sides of the six-metre-long conference table as the Leader presided over the meeting. The engineers began to run that segment of the tape over and over on the wide screen that had been set up on the far side of the room. Everyone came to the same conclusion: the shadow had screwed up by leaving his position, and divine intervention had saved the Leader from falling by placing a quick-thinking person with fast and sure reflexes behind him. Even more important was the fact that this person loved the Leader and was totally dedicated to serving him: it was evident in his unconscious response of catching the Leader at exactly the right moment; it proved his integrity, his qualifications and that he was a reliable person who could be trusted.

The Leader fired his shadow and appointed someone else to replace him. Then he asked for the stumbling scene to be replayed endlessly in slow motion on the closed cir-cuit television at the palace so he could study it nonstop, wherever he went and in whichever direction he looked. Television screens had been installed all over the palace. There was not a room without one: his bedroom and the bathroom, most importantly, where the Leader could be alone with his thoughts. At night when he lay in bed rewatching that stumbling scene, he felt that he liked this person even though he had never met him. What caught his eye and got him addicted to watching the images of his stumble and ensuing rescue was the movement made so casually by that man who had been standing behind him. As soon as the Leader started to fall that person suddenly thrust his hands out underneath the Leader's arms and began to fall down with him. His downward pivot along with the Leader's fall was astonishing, especially in slow motion, and when the two bodies arrived at a certain point the other person's body stopped falling. The two bodies collided and started to rise again by the strength of that other person alone, and once the Leader was returned to his upright position that man's body remained attached to his back for a full three seconds, at which point he pulled away although his hands remained under the Leader's arms. He watched himself twist round even with those two hands still under his arms in order to look that man in the face. At that moment his two hands were retracted from under his arms and the man bowed out of respect. After watching this other man's body and face move in slow motion thousands of times, he came to like him. And when the Leader likes someone it's as if the Night of Excellence, the night the Quran is said to have first been revealed to the Prophet Muhammad, has arrived. His underarms still ached after being grabbed from behind so enthusiastically and his back still remembered the warmth of that man who cleaved to him. He wanted to know who this person was; he wanted to meet him and compensate him. He gave his orders at three o'clock in the morning. By two o'clock that afternoon they had brought the man to see him. The Leader was careful to hold their meeting at an unofficial spot, at the lunch table to be precise.

It is the habit of bodyguards and agents in the security apparatus not to tell a person anything—anything at all— when they take them from their house for a special occasion. This is precisely what happened to Mr Ha'el, and he nearly kissed the hands of those three men who had come for him in his town in order to find out where they were taking him, what the occasion was and what was going to happen to him, but they silently eyed him with discomfiting looks. Silence is their trademark. Besides, any word could cause its utterer to be punished, so Mr Ha'el remained ignorant of what was happening to him. He could do nothing more than tremble and turn yellow, which was the state he was in when they brought him into the Leader's dining room without his even knowing he was on the verge of meeting the Leader himself. Once inside he did not immediately recognize the Leader seated across the table from him, dressed in run-of-the-mill clothes as he chewed his food, believing him to be one of the ordinary bureaucrats instead. In his fear and disorientation he had forgotten what the Leader's face looked like and failed to recognize him until the Leader asked him to come closer. As the Leader got up, wiped his hands and mouth with a napkin, welcomingly shook his hand and invited him to sit to his right in order to have some food with him, Mr Ha'el was the one who nearly collapsed, this time from joy.

The two of them ate and talked for a long time. After learning everything there was to know about Mr Ha'el, the Leader invited him to have some tea in his favourite spot, a glass room filled with flowers and strange plants where they smoked cigars. The Leader asked his assistants to show Mr Ha'el to one of the guest rooms so he could get some rest. In the evening he invited him into his video room to watch a few hours of recordings of the masses chanting for him and killing themselves on his behalf.

This hospitality in the Leader's palace lasted for three days, during which time the two of them ate an inordinate amount of many and varied kinds of food, played backgammon together, swam in the private swimming pool, sat in the sauna, ran around the garden and exercised on the workout equipment in the Leader's private athletic room. In the evening the two of them would watch videos of the masses. On the morning of the fourth day the assistants asked him to meet with the Leader once more before he left. This time he met him in his office, where the Leader asked him which position would allow him to be of the greatest service. Mr Ha'el could not come up with anything other than chief of police in his hometown. The Leader found this suggestion strange and was touched by his friend's modesty. He refused to appoint Mr Ha'el to any position that would take him far away from the capital or from him personally, instead appointing him as head of the apparatus responsible for his own personal security.

My mother waited for me to open my mouth.

"How did you meet him?" I asked.

"It's a long story. Actually I'm a friend of his office manager's wife. She told me he had been asking about me and asked if I had any objections to meeting him. It turns out they had talked the matter over before he ever asked me out for coffee."

"And you said yes?"

"Yes."

"Everybody knows he's married to some woman named Aisha."

"He divorced her. Now that he's a big shot in the government she's no longer right for him."

"Does he know that I don't like them and that they don't like me?"

"He knows you very well and says he's even read some of your work."

"How can you marry someone who mistreated your deceased husband, who even now is messing with your son and keeping him from writing?"

"That was all in the past. As for you, I think you're going to get some powerful backing, that you'll be able to go back to writing for the newspaper."

"I can see you're set on this marriage."

"I'm still a young woman. I deserve this."

"What does Samira think?"

"She doesn't care."

So I'm the only person in this entire family who cares. My mother has forgotten all about how she used to describe them to my father and make up jokes about them. Her "not giving a shit" had caused her to unintentionally fall into line. I saw fit to emulate my sister's approach, so I stood up, getting ready to leave. My mother saw me to the outer door, where, after shoving some money in my hand, she asked me what I thought.

"You can marry anyone you want," I said. "You're a free woman."

"Will you come to the wedding?"

"Do you think you could keep me away from that circus?"

"Circus?"

"When do you plan on having it?"

"The wedding? Ha'el wants it to be on Wednesday."

"In three days? He is in a hurry, but why Wednesday in particular? Why not Thursday?"

"Because he wants to get married on the twentieth anniversary of the Leader coming to power."

"I never dreamt they would occupy my mother's bedroom on that day as well."

"Go think it over and try to get a hold on yourself. You're coming to the wedding whether you like it or not. You're my only son. I'd simply die of shame if you weren't there. Anyway, I'll figure out the best way for you two to meet beforehand. I'll give you a call."

"Do you love him?"

"Not yet, he's just a fiancé."

Just a fiancé? As I stared at her, she seemed weaker, lonelier. Here was this amazing woman thinking about marriage in spite of all those wrinkles on her neck and her face. She wanted to get married in order to prove to herself first and foremost that she was still a young woman. I wanted her to be happy. She stretched her neck and offered me her cheek, which I kissed and then left.

CHAPTER THREE

I T WAS A LITTLE past eleven fifteen when I made
it back out into the street. I walked along the pavement even though there was no traffic on the asphalt
road, instinctively making my way downtown, where I
saw hordes of human beings occupying the squares and
the main streets. I could hear the sounds of the march
coming out of television sets in homes nearby. The Leader
has a straightforward rule: housewives not taking part in
the march must watch it on TV. People have to raise the
sound on their sets and leave the windows open if they
do not wish to be accused of being unpatriotic. The poet
had finished reciting his poem and the announcer moved
on to describe the feelings of the masses, their patriotism
and love for the Leader.

"Hark, O Leader, at the mass of masses, how they chant
your name with strength and determination until their
chants reach the clouds in the sky so that your name can
embrace the stars. If there are any other life forms in the
universe we'll find them chanting your name too, chanting
with their faces upturned towards our God-given homeland.
Observe, O Leader, how the masses thank God for having
been born in your era. The Era of Dignity and Freedom.
The Era of the Leader. So lead us, O Leader, lead us to

victory. This is what the masses chant. Lead us to incomparable victory!"

The broadcaster's raspy voice blended in with the chanting and the brass band music being broadcast through megaphones lining the squares and the streets, rousing the enthusiasm of the masses.

Ever since the Leader took power music had been transformed into a national art. There is no longer *l'art pour l'art*. Even those rare intellectuals who were once seen on television and heard over the radio began to assault the theory of *l'art pour l'art*. Music is not for savouring, for burnishing the soul and improving the self; it is not for contemplating or luxuriating the senses; it is for the purposes of enthusiasm alone. "Music must play its role in stirring up the masses," the Leader says. Therefore classical Arabic music and the *muwashahat* are relegated to the back rows, replaced with military marches. What we call authentic art vanishes in the marching crowds, the pounding drums and the screeching horns. Nothing can be heard out of that noise except for the sound of military brass bands, as the instruments of the Arabic orchestra get lost in the shuffle. They have no place in our present. The *kamanche*? A silly and worthless instrument when played to the beating of drums. The same is true for the *qanun* and the *nay*. The *nay* or the horn? The *nay* is insignificant, reactionary and unpatriotic because it drives the listener to contemplation and sorrow, befitting the silence of the grave, whereas the horn renders people more awake and enthusiastic, more patriotic because they will be ready to sacrifice spirit and blood on behalf of the Leader.

But who ever said that military marches are not art? Tchaikovsky is considered one of the greatest composers of the nineteenth century and he wrote a piece entitled 'Slavonic March' in which the music swells to a crescendo at the moment of victory. The very same Tchaikovsky also wrote the '1812 Overture', which is the year that witnessed Napoleon's defeat in Russia. Meanwhile the German musical giant Beethoven wrote his Third Symphony (the *Eroica*) and dedicated it to Napoleon Bonaparte. These symphonies are based on the rhythm of the heroic military march so loved by the Leader. When the Russian Ambassador learned of the Leader's passion (for music), he invited him to Moscow at once, packing his schedule with trips to the Bolshoi and other theatres, where both the Seventh Symphony (Leningrad) and the Eighth Symphony (Stalingrad) by Shostakovich were performed for him.

After the Leader staged his coup twenty years ago the first thing he did was to occupy the radio station and force them to interrupt their programming in order to broadcast military marches. Those marches still remind him of that glorious day. State functionaries always make sure to whistle them while they march or carry out their tasks—see one of them as his cheeks expand and contract to the rhythm of the marches that he recalls in his mind; now imagine him as he purses his lips and blows, imitating the horn.

In reality they are emulating the Leader, who has become accustomed to whistling marches. Those who whistle sappy love songs have no place in the Leader's entourage. What good does it do for the radio to play songs about romance and infatuation? It's pointless, really, and just makes the masses more frustrated. If it ever became necessary to play a song about love, it would have to be a song about love for the Leader. All feelings must be oriented towards the Leader. Love, ardour and rapture, infatuation and affection, passion and ecstasy: they must all be reserved for the Leader. Wasting such emotions on a worthless young woman is nothing less than moral decay itself. Abandonment and estrangement, heartsick weeping on ruins, isolation and death—all are strictly taboo because they could be understood as unpatriotic. Estrangement could be misconstrued as coming between the masses and the Leader or be taken to mean that the masses have given up on their Leader—God forbid—so such words have passed out of popular music. For those who stay up past one in the morning one song was permitted just before the television signed off for the night, 'Up Late Alone' by Umm Kulthum, but it could only be played on the condition that a picture of the Leader appeared at the same time. Even staying up late must be on the Leader's behalf, in order to secretly confide in his image, or else. But citizens should not stay up late. They should go to bed early with the goal of waking up in the morning to get a fresh start in order to build the homeland with ardour and vigour under the inspirational leadership of the Leader.

I heard a car approaching from behind me but I didn't turn around because I could tell by the rev of the engine that it was being driven in a herky-jerky manner, a hallmark of the military security goons. My intuition did not fail me. The clumsy driver slammed on the brakes and the car screeched to a halt beside me. It was one of their unmarked cars, which they would drive around without any number plates. Three goons in civilian clothes hopped out of the back seat wielding machine guns. Their stubbly chins, rumpled clothes and bodies reeking of sweat gave them away. They looked as if they had just been awakened from troubled sleep. I did not stop for them the way that a citizen is expected to do. Instead, I kept walking and made them hurry after me, calling, "Stop... I'm coming... for you!!" I stopped, and by the time the three of them surrounded me, I noticed women and children were watching us from their windows.

"What do you want?" I asked.

"Come see the boss for a minute," one of them said.

He was referring to the olive-skinned man with a thick moustache sitting in the passenger seat. The boss watched me with inquisitive eyes as I moved closer. The three goons surrounded me, placing me at the centre of a triangle. The boss addressed me from inside the car. One of the three goons squeezed my neck and forced me to bend down to the window.

"What are you doing around here?"

"Just visiting someone in the neighbourhood."

"And who is this someone?"

"My mother."

"Why aren't you at the march?"

"I'm not an employee or a student, not a Party member or a union rep, not..."

"Identification," they said, interrupting me abruptly.

"Some Comrades took it away from me about an hour ago."

"Name."

"Fathi Sheen."

He raised his eyes towards me, stared at me hard and demanded, "The writer, Fathi Sheen?"

"Yeah, that's right."

Switching on the walkie-talkie and moving it to his ear, he told me, "You ought to be ashamed of yourself."

"Why's that?"

"Don't talk back when the boss is talking to you," one of the three upbraided me.

The boss made a gesture and two of the three men yanked me away from the window. Apparently he didn't want me to hear the conversation he was conducting in a hushed voice. From the movement of his lips I could see him mention my name more than once. After he switched off the walkie-talkie they moved me back closer to him. He remained silent for a moment and then said, without looking at me, "You have to come down to military security at nine o'clock."

He gestured to his men to let me go and they got back inside the car. Before they took off I asked him, "What about my ID?"

"You can sort out your situation with the Comrades later on."

The car raced off like a shot, leaving streaked tyre marks on the asphalt. I looked up and spotted the same eyes watching what was going on before the women and children retreated further inside. What is it this morning? I asked myself. I'm already mixed up with the Comrades, now military security too?

The roar from the television sets grew louder as the masses began to shout with intense enthusiasm for some reason or another. The announcer nearly broke out in tears from all the emotion. I felt bad for not being at my mother's or at Lama's watching what was happening. By the way, I haven't had a television ever since I gave mine to one of my friends as a wedding present. I don't regret that at all. I got rid of it because I got bored with all the marches and the Leader's speeches, with everything they show nonstop.

I walked towards the streets that were clogged with the masses and that divide the city in two. I had to get over to the other side where Lama lives. With every step I took the roar in the atmosphere grew louder. It was the very same roar I heard coming from everyone's television. I think the sudden shouting of the masses was due to the Leader's surprise appearance. He would often come out to greet the people unexpectedly, sending them into a bizarre tizzy.

You ought to be ashamed of yourself. Why had the military security officer said that? In order to answer that question, let me tell you a bit about myself before I get to Lama's.

Lama and I love each other but we have not got married yet. Even though we both want to, Lama is still tied up with the consequences of her previous marriage. Her husband, a businessman, refuses to finalize their divorce despite the fact that they have been separated for many years. One time he went on a business trip to Asia. When he came back Lama had a dream that caused her to wake up in a panic. She dreamt he had not been on a business trip at all but had gone on a honeymoon with a second wife whom he had married in secret and who was actually his personal secretary. When she woke up, though, she found him deep asleep next to her, exhausted from the sex they had just had. She found it curious that he had not been up for it at first (despite his long absence and her caresses that I know are amazing and can make iron weep), but after several attempts she finally wore both of them down. Apparently the sex disoriented her and helped her subconscious mind discover the reason why, by driving her to have that dream. She dreamt that he and his secretary were having a beautiful honeymoon on a Spanish beach. Naked, she got out of bed and searched his pockets for his passport. On a page that was covered with entry and exit stamps she found a Spanish visa. The Spanish exit stamp was for the day he had returned home and the same night they had had sex. That night she slept on the couch in the living room and in the morning she confronted him with what she had discovered. He denied it at first but eventually confessed that he actually had married his secretary, pleading that he had had no choice in the matter because she was the niece of a senior Party Comrade and marrying her was going to help him take care of business affairs more quickly, instead of getting bogged down in routine, denial and delay.

Lama was not going to let a second wife share her husband. Anyway, her husband had betrayed her, stabbed her in the back. She grew to hate him, which made it impossible for her to live under the same roof with him, and so she went to live with her family for a while until she finally bought a flat on a quiet side street on the other side of town using money she had saved in a private bank account. During the same year in which Lama was liberated, my father died, and I moved out to live in my own flat (which my mother had bought for me). That was when the anger of the government came crashing down upon me.

At one point during that year, while I was in the studio getting ready to record my weekly literary programme on Channel One, the producer's assistant came in and handed me a scrap of paper from the station's administration asking me to stop recording at once and to come immediately to a meeting with the director of cultural programming, who handed me another piece of paper, which he had received by fax from one of the security services and which criticized my programme because I had not mentioned the Leader recently. As I slowly read the note I felt myself approaching a crossroads. I sipped my cup of coffee and smoked in order to buy myself some time. I had to look out for my daily bread but at the same time my reputation as an independent writer was on the line. My programme discussed recently published books and for each episode I would meet a writer to talk about his or her new book. The programme also used to hold short-story and poetry contests, earning the respect of writers and viewers alike because of my insistence on integrity and on applying standards with precision and neutrality.

I asked the programming director what he thought I should do and he proposed holding a contest for stories and poetry about the Leader and his accomplishments. I refused. Straight away and without asking why he asked me to hand in my resignation, claiming that every television programme, no matter what, should be true to the principles and the person of the Leader. I wrote out my resignation, signed it and handed it over to the station's administration. Then I went back down to the studio. As I said goodbye to the director and the technicians I received a phone call from the administration informing me that, pursuant to my request, they had accepted my resignation. They didn't stop there, though; they wanted me to give up journalism and literature altogether. Misfortunes and obstacles fell down on me once they decided to stop mentioning my name or my works in all the national media. Later a directive was sent to the censorship committees with the order not to approve any new publication of mine, not even if it were a children's book. Finally they expelled me from the writers' and journalists' union, claiming I owed two years' worth of back dues. They ordered some Comrade writers to attack my books and slander me personally, calling me the "unpatriotic" writer because I had insulted the Inspirer of the Nation and the Compass of Humanity, as they put it. It came to my attention that one of the writers—Comrades all—who had been brought together for a conference on some national holiday or another got up and shouted for my downfall. Some of his colleagues joined in, spasmodically shouting, *Down, Down, Down!*

And so I was brought down. But I won Lama, who started to hate the Comrades and love their victims because her husband had stabbed her in the back by secretly marrying one of their nieces just to serve his business interests. Lama and I had met at the house of a poet friend of mine, one who had also refused to write poems glorifying the Leader, by the way, and so was blacklisted too. When Lama walked in I felt as though the two of us had come to our mutual poet friend's house precisely in order to meet. We talked alone in the corner. She asked me what was new and told me how she used to watch my television show and that she read one of my books. When I told her I had stopped writing, she grew intrigued and launched a barrage of questions at me in order to find out exactly why I had stopped. At that point she asked me to walk her home and we ended up strolling for two hours, talking about everything except her problems. I could feel her sympathy for me. The next day I visited my poet friend again to ask him about her and he told me the story of her businessman husband and his secretary, the Party Comrade's niece.

Her husband resisted getting a divorce because he claimed to still love her so much that he would even be willing to divorce the secretary if she would come back to him. Lama refused and told him that she was in love with me and that we were planning to get married just as soon as the divorce went through. The fire of jealousy was ignited inside him and he became more and more stubborn. One day he phoned to tell me he wanted to meet. We had coffee in a hotel coffee shop and I tried to convince him to end the matter amicably, that this was in everyone's best interests, but in return he threatened me by saying that he could orchestrate a terrible situation for me with the regime if I did not stay away from his wife. He was hinting at his second wife's uncle's influence but I scoffed and said, "Fuck you, and fuck the Party." He warned me that I would pay dearly for what I had just said and took off. When I told Lama what had happened she laughed for a long time and I laughed too. To this day, whenever we're together, we still laugh whenever the Party is mentioned.

Actually the security services summoned me more than once for questioning about the insult I had directed towards the Party. I confessed to uttering that word but said that I hated having to use it and that I only said it because the businessman had provoked me. The businessman had filed an ambiguous report, citing the insult without clarifying whether I had directed it at the Leader personally or just the Party in general. The security services became very interested in this dust-up: Had I meant just the Party or both the Leader and the Party together? There's a difference, of course. Insulting the Leader can land a person in prison for twenty years whereas insulting the Party is no major crime. I insisted that I had meant the Party alone because the secretary's uncle is an influential delegate. The second time I reported to see them at nine a.m., and I waited for hours on end until an interrogator came to deal with me. As soon as one investigator finished up they would transfer me to another. Every one of them would add his signature to the file because they all had to investigate the matter individually from start to finish. They would ask me, "How can an intellectual and a writer use such a word?" The funny thing about the whole situation was that the word got repeated so many times at headquarters they started calling me "Mr Fuck" and every investigator who looked into the subject became "Inspector Fuck". One time an investigator asked me how to spell the word, whether it was written with a "c" or with a "k".

I apologize to the reader for repeating this word but "Fuck-Gate" really wore me out, the obvious hilarity notwithstanding. I would go see Lama as soon as I left the *mukhabarat* building. My poor dear would be waiting for me by the window, on tenterhooks, exposing herself to the blazing sunlight. As soon as she saw me coming she would hurry to open the door and hold me for fifteen minutes, trembling. When I finally managed to peel myself away from her, I would take her to bed and undress her. Once we were spent Lama would calmly take me to the bathroom, giggling, and I would let her wash my body because she loved doing that so much. In the end we would head back to bed soaking wet so I could tell her all about what had happened to me there and we would have a good laugh about it.

We used to take revenge on our situation through laughter but laughter is accursed chattering that only exposes us and gets us into uncomfortable situations. One time we were at a wake for a friend of ours, a writer, who had passed away after a long battle with illness. Lama and I went because we felt, justifiably so, how horrible it was to lose this friend whom Lama had visited at his house every day in order to help care for him. Like a nurse she would wipe his body down with cologne, change his clothes and bedsheets and feed him by hand. When the illness got really bad we were forced to move him to the public hospital, where Lama insisted on staying with him, sleeping on chairs in the waiting room; she would wake up and find herself covered in tears. When he died I had to stay with her in order to calm her down. She was not strong enough to keep herself from

69

crying. This woman would often cry at the mere sight of a miserable cat but her mood turned around 180 degrees at the wake the writers' union held on the occasion of the *arbaeen* of our friend the writer.

The Leader's father was killed at the age of eighty-two when his private plane was returning to the homeland after a vacation in Monte Carlo and crashed. It was a horrible accident that shook the entire nation and brought unhappiness upon its citizens; music and comedy were banned from the media and every meeting had to begin with a standing moment of silence in order to honour the soul of "the old man". At the wake, the Lieutenant Colonel came up to the front and asked everyone to stand for a moment of silence (everybody assumed he was asking us to stand in order to honour the soul of our beloved friend and writer so we all got up before he could even finish his sentence) and intoned, "to honour the soul of the Leader's father".

We had just stood up when we realized we were standing out of respect for the soul of the Leader's father and not the soul of our friend. I got upset and glowered. As the minute turned into several minutes and the matter did not seem to concern the Leader, I could tell, even with my eyes shut, that Lama was beginning to vibrate. I assumed she was crying but when I looked over I saw she was trying to keep herself from laughing. She was red in the face and shaking and had covered her mouth with her hand. The virus of laughter spread to me too and I started to suck hard on the inner walls of my mouth until I suppressed it. Luckily the moment of silence only lasted 180 seconds. Once we were asked to be seated Lama kneeled down between the rows of chairs to avoid blurting out that wave of laughter that had washed over her. Thankfully the situation ended well.

The speakers started taking their turns up at the dais, praising the departed, his humanity, his good manners and his spirit. But they added something else as well, claiming that the departed had been a devoted Party member. They must have mentioned the Party a dozen times and every time she heard the Party mentioned Lama would cover her mouth and drop her head and shake, and I would immediately follow her lead and do the same. Remembering that word, she would think about how the mention of it had brought me in to be questioned at the security branch. We had to leave before the wake was over because when Lama gets giggly nobody can stop her from laughing. In fact, as soon as we walked out the door she burst out laughing as the people watched us in bewilderment.

I hope the reader now understands why the military security agent said what I have been told hundreds of times over the past five years: *You ought to be ashamed of yourself.* Some people use the word treasonous to describe me just like that Comrade did more than two hours ago, when I dared to stand up for the young man as they beat him senseless. They may tell me I'm a traitor but I'm not ashamed for refusing to stage a contest for short stories and poetry about the Leader on my television show or for telling Lama's ex-husband "Fuck the Party".

CHAPTER FOUR

A FTER HAVING WALKED under the blazing sun all the way from the neighbourhood where my mother lives, I felt a refreshing coolness as soon as I set foot inside Lama's building. Public transportation was not running, even in neighbourhoods far away from the flow of the enormous human stream that is the march. They had cut back services, as always, assuming that everyone is either at the march or at home watching it on TV. Buses sat parked with their doors shut; drivers had been hauled off to the celebrations. There must have been hundreds of them, parked in several rows on the streets, waiting until the march was finished so they could take all the rural folk back to their villages and towns whence they had been brought early this morning.

As I cooled off I felt slightly invigorated though I failed to recover the peace of mind I had lost this morning as Lama's neighbours' television sets blared at unusually high levels in order to satisfy the Comrades and the goons, turned up so loud that the women and children could not help but watch the marching masses even when they were hunkered down in their own homes. As I climbed the steps, and the whole way over there in fact, I could hear the shouting and the roar of the masses—a perpetual state of agitation I could not quite comprehend. Through their doors I could hear the building's residents commenting enthusiastically about what they saw.

Lama opened the door for me and I walked straight into hell. The flat was sweltering. She was wearing nothing but a bikini, reviving herself with water from time to time. She was moist with sweat and her skin glistened. She seemed edgy, on the verge of breaking down into tears; to keep her from doing so I embraced her reassuringly, holding her close. She told me she had started getting nervous after trying to call me several times. She hadn't imagined that I would dare to go outside on such a terrible day. She could have stayed like that for an hour, as we held each other behind the door; it calmed her down... but I pulled away, took her by the hand and helped her onto the couch, sitting down beside her in front of the TV. I was fascinated to know what it was that could send the masses into such hysterics. She nearly choked me with her arms, burying her face in my chest while I watched the screen.

The masses had been transformed from a patchwork of multiple currents, each one led by someone chanting through a hand-held megaphone as the group repeated the same chant, into a single torrent spanning several kilometres. The camera could not capture the full extent of the stream. The square was packed with people and pictures of the Leader. The agglomeration swelled as those human waves surged like the sea, forming an endless undulating chain. Many people had climbed up trees and streetlights and traffic lights, filling the balconies and the rooftops as the roar reached a crescendo alongside the military march and the voices of the commentators and the shouting of the masses. As I noticed everyone's attention being drawn to the balconies in the hotel overlooking the square, something happened, and the people began madly shouting and hollering. I peered closer and saw a ghost resembling the Leader appear every once in a while in one of the windows overlooking the square... slowing down a bit, just enough so the masses could recognize him, and then disappearing. Whenever his ghost appeared the people would holler and scream. As they hollered, the camera would carefully zoom in on the people's faces in one particular area before panning to another. When the ghost of the Leader appeared they would thrust their hands up towards him and shout at the top of their lungs—mouths open as wide as possible, neck veins bulging, nerves on edge, faces damp with sweat as they turned red (and oh, what sweat it was, as if the masses had just emerged from the ocean). All of a sudden, a bodyguard came out onto the balcony holding a statue of the Leader high above his head, displaying it in all directions as the masses hollered relentlessly, their shouts reaching farther and farther, like the call of a bird as it flies away. This statue presentation lasted for five minutes until he disappeared and the wave of shouting died down bit by bit until it was nearly extinguished. But the Leader had no intention of letting the masses calm down. Just then his ghost appeared from behind the window and the shouting started back up all over again.

With her arms wrapped round me Lama whispered that I was neglecting her.

"Sweetie."

"Yes, Lama?"

"What's so important about that circus? I've never known you to be so interested."

I stroked her hair so she would let me keep watching for a few more minutes. Pretending to be asleep, she whispered, "Turn it off... please."

"Just a minute, my love. I'm right here. Just one minute."

"I'm bored."

"One more minute."

"Your clothes are completely soaked with sweat."

"I'll take them off in a little while."

"Do you want me to do it for you?"

Without waiting for a response she started undoing my buttons, drowsily, pressing her nose in close to my body to smell it, as if she were on drugs. I let her do whatever she wanted even as the Leader continued toying with the masses. I wanted to bear witness to this strangest of relationships between the Leader and the masses.

The Leader had become accustomed to playing with the masses, to toying with them. Ordinarily he would be late showing up to a mass convergence or a celebration organized in his honour. Every time the crowd would anticipate his appearance at any moment, except on occasions when he was busy and would send someone else in his stead, turning all the preparations into a waste. Or just the opposite: he might appear at times when he was unexpected. He had made an art out of stunning the people, and he would laugh out loud whenever he saw those signs of awe on people's faces. One time he sent his youngest son to inaugurate a charity market. The presence of the son is enough to warrant the same kind of pomp and ceremony that calls for masses who will chant the Leader's name and a brass band and reception by state functionaries. On the day the charity market was inaugurated, the governor had a gift for the little boy, a decorated horse that he could ride and that would bring him joy. The procession arrived, the people chanted and the band started to play a military march as fireworks were set off overhead... and just then the red Mercedes that the son typically rode in stopped and the Leader himself stepped out instead. What a surprise it was, tying everyone's tongues, but the shock only lasted a few seconds until the Leader was received as he must be, and the absence of the son was forgotten. The Governor presented the Leader with the horse that had been decorated in a manner that would please children, and he accepted it, laughing to his aides.

Meanwhile, on another occasion to dedicate a water purification facility, the son unexpectedly stepped off the train that the father was supposed to be on. In such moments the Leader toyed with the enormous torrent of the masses in new and previously unheard-of ways. He behaved like a child. What else should one call passing by a window like that, stopping for a moment before disappearing and then dispatching one's assistants out onto the balcony to show the masses a statue and then pictures of oneself in different outfits?

I made Lama's task easier by lifting myself up off the couch as she removed my last piece of clothing. At that moment one of the Leader's assistants came out carrying a model draped in the Leader's military uniform, adorned with all the medals and badges he had earned, and then proceeded to turn the model in every direction as the state of excitement reached an even higher, unprecedentedly high level. Hands were raised as though they wanted to reach out and touch the uniform. The television producer cut to a shot of scores of young women jumping up and down, screaming and weeping. That scene reminded me of audiences at rock concerts in the West, where young ladies are struck with comparable hysteria. They do the exact same thing here. Women were reaching out their hands and screaming as tears streamed down their cheeks... some of them held their heads as they screamed.

I stroked Lama's hair as her mouth wandered round my chest. She now sat on the couch so she could rest her knees as she devoured my body. It was her habit to moan as she caressed me, not the way a woman moans from ecstasy but as though she were complaining, complaining about something with muted moans that emanated from a tortured soul. In that moment I could feel her moaning through her touch but I could not actually hear her because of the loud television. She whispered in my ear and then sucked it in her mouth, "Turn off the television... please."

"Just a minute, I want to see where this madness ends up."

"Screw them," she said, kneading my chest. When I let out a brief laugh she brought her mouth down below, preceded by her hand. She was trying every means to convince me to switch off the television. But how could I? At that moment they were lowering another one of the Leader's uniforms with ropes so that the masses could touch it. Hands were outstretched and people started leaping up just to graze its edge. The shouting grew louder and a segment of the masses torqued in a terrifying manner. At one particular moment the uniform was quickly whisked away and as it vanished the Leader himself appeared. Madness reigned over all existence.

A theatrical move that not even Aristotle himself imagined in his *Politics*, where he elaborated on the deification of the king in the East.

The Greeks became familiar with the nature of rule in the East when Alexander the Great conquered the lands of Persia in the fourth century BC. After the celebrated conqueror returned to Athens he wanted to emulate the Shahs of Persia by imposing their custom of deifying themselves, specifically in the form of the relationship between ruler and ruled. Whereas that relationship in Athens had been between the ruler and the citizen, in the East it was an expression of the relationship between the god-king and the slave. People in the lands of Persia would prostrate themselves before their kings and it was this in particular that Alexander the Great wanted to implement in his own country, but he met with the opposition of the Macedonians. The important thing is that the Macedonians refused to deify their kings and to lie down before them, while the people of the East agreed to do so without any discussion. Whether in Persia or Egypt or China, kings were deities and human beings were slaves. This refusal among the Macedonians was the opposite of a state of total acceptance among the inhabitants of the East. As a result tyranny became bound up in the Western mind as the Eastern condition, and for that reason Aristotle went on at great length about Eastern tyranny, describing it and philosophizing about it.

Human beings in the East are happy slaves, to the point that Hegel believed: "In the East only one individual is free: the despot." It follows that whosoever is not a despot must be a slave. Aristotle advised his student Alexander to adhere to two styles in governing the lands extending from the East to the West: think of human beings in Macedonia as citizens and consider Asians slaves. Therefore, the people of Persia were made to lie prostrate before Alexander the Great while those outside of Asia were exempted from doing so. He minted money using the word *shah* to describe himself in Persia, even more specifically, "The Lion Slayer". Matters degenerated still further after that as kingship—as it was called—became firmly implanted in the Hellenistic world and the *shah* grew unfettered: becoming the lawgiver and a leader more powerful than the army and the highest judicial authority; omniscient, he behaved however he wished, giving whatever orders he desired and so forth and so on. At some point the West became afflicted with tyranny. Its origin: the East.

As I was saying, the Macedonians refused to deify Alexander despite the fact that he was a great conqueror who achieved splendid victories for his country. Consider this irony, dear reader, that as soon as Alexander entered the lands of Persia as a conqueror the people deified him whereas the people of his own tribe condemned that deification and pushed back against it. History records one of his generals mockingly laughing out loud when he heard of this trend towards deification that Alexander the Great had been preparing to impose on them. Alexander imagined they were making fun of him and he felt rebuffed. But that did not eliminate the thought from his mind altogether; rather, he said the Asians had no objection and that he was like a god to them and they were his happy and willing slaves.

We are willing slaves and the proof is in what was going on just a little while ago in the large plaza outside the hotel, where the Leader was toying with the people (the slaves) to the point that he sent out his military uniforms and his medals in order to make them go mad just by touching them. He loves to see the masses kill themselves on his behalf. As I walked over to Lama's flat I saw more than one ambulance speed off silently, transporting whoever had been overwhelmed—and there were many of them in that crowd and that heat. One time a doctor informed me, asking to remain anonymous, that in every march like this one more than a hundred people die, whether trampled or suffocated, and twice that number would die in traffic accidents as people returned to their homes and villages.

Why does the Leader love these marches so? Hannah Arendt discussed the relationship between the Leader and the masses, coming to the conclusion that the masses cannot live without a Leader, just as the Leader cannot live without masses. In other words, the Leader cannot exist without the masses just as there is no existence for the masses without the Leader—two poles, each one cannot exist without the existence of the other. We're not talking about the individual people who constitute the masses here now, but about masses of humanity, hordes of human beings who constitute the masses and who can be found at a particular time in a particular place chanting for the Leader. I believe the Leader loses his self-confidence and gets depressed when too much time passes without him seeing the masses fill the streets in order to chant his name. As I already mentioned, the Leader regularly watched video clips of the masses chanting for him in marches or in crowded gatherings. He would do this in the interim between one march and the next, between one crowded gathering and another. I would venture to say that he does this in order to avoid losing his self-confidence. He had a habit of inviting guests into his video room in order to watch hours of those clips. I trust the reader will recall that he had invited over Mr Ha'el, who wants to marry my mother, in order to watch these tapes. Television screens re-airing the most recent march fill out every corner of the Leader's palace.

After one of the gigantic marches held on the occasion of independence, in which the masses had been chanting for the Leader and nobody else (in spite of the fact that the Leader had only been a little boy when the foreign armies were evacuated), a grave error took place and the entire recording was lost. How did that happen? God only knows. There are some who say it was a premeditated act while others say that the technician made a mistake, using the original recording instead of a blank cassette and taping over its contents! What matters is that the Minister of Communications had to accompany the television producer to the palace in order to explain the situation to the Leader, who flipped his lid and whomped the producer with an ashtray instead of responding. I don't know why the Leader got so upset. All the marches are the same and he could have found his own way to get over it, say, by sitting in the video room watching the previous march, for example. Also, the Minister and the TV producer proved to be "two stupid arses" because they could have saved

face by simply handing over a recording of an earlier
march since all of our marches are essentially the same.
I swear the Leader would not be able to tell the difference. They are nothing but shrieking masses: the roar, the
military march music and images of the Leader that are
more numerous than the number of those stuffed into
the streets and the plazas. It was a good throw but the
ashtray didn't strike the TV producer in the head, hitting
him in the shoulder instead. Fearing that the Leader was
about to fire them both, the Minister suggested that he
and the producer restage the march, which could be held
one week after the anniversary of independence. The idea
impressed the Leader and he made the necessary orders.
The march was rescheduled and videotaped and now the
Leader has a copy in his library.

After a vigorous effort they were able to quieten the
masses, which had carried on shouting and hollering for a
long time, hypnotized by the scene the Leader had success-
fully orchestrated when he appeared after toying with them.
Everyone on the balcony was gesturing for the masses to be
silent. Apparently the Leader had something he wanted to
say on this occasion. An unexpected silence fell that attracted
Lama, who had been busy caressing me. Despite the fact
that I had not reciprocated Lama's advances and did not
respond to her caresses except by getting erect as I followed
everything that was happening on television, I felt utterly
disconnected from what was happening as a result of that
silence; in the wake of the roar that had been pounding
my ears came this silence, and I was split in two. I could
not tear my eyes away from the television to cast a glance

at Lama's head or follow what she was doing. Instead I was like someone under hypnosis, staring at the screen where the Leader appeared, preparing to open his mouth. But I was separated from all of that. I felt a mixture of pleasures: one was emanating from my loins; another was due to the interruption of the long roar and the onset of ringing that soon quieted down and grew softer in my ears; and one final pleasure was due to my separation from that world. Lama suddenly noticed the silence and raised her head. She wanted to know the reason for the silence and she saw how, at that very moment, the Leader made certain that the masses were ready to listen to what he had to say, so he opened his mouth to speak... but no! As though he had forgotten what he wanted to say, his mouth hung agape. At once she was swept away by a powerful fit of laughter that jolted me out of my condition, reconnecting me with reality here. I asked her what had happened that could make her burst out laughing like that.

We switched off the television and sprawled out on the couch. The Leader's voice continued assaulting us from outside, from all sides, from the direction of the stairwell, from the street. The stairwell annoyingly amplified sound, as if the television were still on.

The fan was spinning on its highest setting but all that did was recirculate hot air. We were naked and our bodies were drenched with sweat. In order to stay cool Lama would go into the bathroom every fifteen minutes and stand in the shower for a moment, returning to roll around on top of me and then get up so I could feel a blast of air blowing from the fan and enjoy some coolness. She would also moisten a towel and wipe down my body. Because of the layout of her flat Lama had to invent new means to fight the heat, which included filling up plastic bags with water, tying them in a knot, placing them in the freezer and then bringing them out once they were frozen in order to slide them all over me, from my head down to my feet. I felt the pleasure of coolness most on my head and feet whereas on the rest of my skin I felt the sting of iciness that was no different than the sting of hotness. I preferred the wet towel that she rubbed all over my body as the fan spun and blew air at me. She made sure not to let my penis get so cold that it went limp. From the warmth and the hot air and our sweaty bodies and the game of physical cooling Lama used to play, some sort of desire would eventually pop out and we would make love. Lama came to learn how much I hate physical contact in that sweaty atmosphere. As soon as she stopped cooling us down with her special methods we would become completely soaked with sweat and our bodies would get all slimy. I recoil from the contact of two slimy, sticky bodies but Lama loves it and yearns for it all the time. Mostly I put up with it in order to satisfy her.

The whole operation went on longer than usual because of the Leader's speech, which was coming through the doors and the walls to reach us in a clear and comprehensible voice. I got distracted whenever I heard him say a particular word or phrase, either rebutting him or repeating the word to myself in order to understand what he meant by it, but what distracted me the most were his grammatical mistakes. I discovered that he likes to assimilate subject and object although he could apply the circumstantial *hal* construction in an excellent manner and without making any mistakes. Among his other grammatical errors: misvowelling the possessed element in a possessive *idafa* construction or confusing the nominal sentence with the verbal sentence, so instead of saying "the liberation of the country", he might say, "liberation, the country". These mistakes distracted me, even when Lama and I were making love. And while I corrected the Leader's grammatical mistakes in my mind, distant from what we were actually doing, Lama was passionately trying to come! Her panting and moaning would bring me back but soon I would drift away once again on account of a particular word or another grammatical mistake. In the moment when I heard the Leader defame the president of a neighbouring country, the masses exploded into shouting and hollering and clapping as Lama shuddered and screamed out several short yelps before quieting down with a smile on her face.

Lama's bathroom is remarkably tranquil despite the fact that it has a small window overlooking the roof of the adjacent building; by tranquillity I don't mean that when we fill the bathtub with water and sit in it that the Leader's voice giving his speech can't reach us but that it would reach us in a more muffled way, like some distant, unintelligible murmur. That noise did not prevent me from staying focused on Lama as she sat down on the edge of the tub. She berated herself for being so selfish and for being incapable of making me happy. I told her that the Leader's speech and all the day's noise were what kept me from being happy; then I told her about everything that had happened to me from the moment I left the house in the morning until my arrival at her place. Confused, she asked me, "Did you say Mr Ha'el?"

"That's right. My mother's going to marry Mr Ha'el, that man who is now one of the closest people to the Leader."

"Do you realize what you're saying?"

"I know exactly what I'm saying. I was just over at my mother's place and she told me the two of them are going to get married on Wednesday, in just three days, on the Leader's twentieth anniversary. Mr Ha'el wants to make a good impression on the Leader by getting married on the day of his anniversary."

"How did she meet him?"

"She talked about female arrangements."

"That Mr Ha'el is a strange one. He knows for sure that you're her son and that they hate you very much. I once overheard somebody say that the only reason you're still alive is because you're a well-known writer. Otherwise they would have got rid of you. You hate them as well so tell me, what kind of a marriage is this? And don't tell me you're going!"

"My mother says she's still a young woman, that she deserves to get married. Besides, her friend who is the wife of the director of Mr Ha'el's office arranged the whole thing. Don't ask me to answer questions like that. I don't know how to respond."

"You don't know how to respond to me about whether or not you're going to the wedding?"

"I'll answer you about that of course. She asked me to come because she wants me there by her side. Without me she'd feel ashamed. Do you want to come with me? We'll have fun."

She stared hard at me for a long time in order to figure out whether I was serious. She didn't completely believe what I said, and that was justified; I was in disbelief myself. Her severe response caused me to doubt the soundness of my own calm. Was I unaware of some danger aimed right at me? Should I have been angry or afraid? With a sure tongue she said, "I see you're calm and at peace."

"Actually, I am calm and at peace."

"Aren't you afraid they might be planning some kind of a trap for you?"

"Like what? Tell me, please."

She was upset with me. She got out of the tub as water dripped from her shimmering body. She didn't pick up a towel and try to cover up her nudity as she usually would when she was upset. I loved her arse, which shook abruptly as water flew from it. When she turned back to glance at me before leaving the bathroom she caught me staring at her from behind. She stopped at the bathroom door, spun round and leaned one hand against the wall, wrapped the other one around her waist and shifted all her weight to one leg as she bent the other one and placed it on her toes—it was a special and amazing position. Her anger turned into a sly smile even as water dripped from her pubic hair. Slowly, enunciating carefully, she asked, "Can we talk about this outside the bathroom, please?"

"Where?"

"The living room."

"Will you stand like that out there, too? You're unbelievable in that pose."

She laughed softly, leaning her head to one side and hiding her face behind her raised forearm. Her anger dissipated. No matter what, in both states, Lama is gorgeous.

"All right, I'll follow you," I told her, getting up out of the tub.

I didn't want to ruin her couch so I dried off bit-by-bit, running the towel quickly over my body, which holds more water than Lama's because of my enormity and the hair that blankets me. When I emerged from the bathroom I found her sitting on the couch, one knee bent up next to her as she rested her head against the edge of the couch. The beautiful thing about Lama is that she isn't bashful about being naked around me. She is completely open and reveals everything about herself to me. I sat down on the end of the couch she left open for me and rested my arm and head the way she had done. I noticed a thin layer of tears in her eyes, which meant that she was seriously distressed and anxious, so I decided not to mess with her.

"Do you have any idea that they're ganging up on you in order to win you over?" she asked. "Now they're intermarrying to get to you. They want you back in their clutches once and for all."

"But I've been silent all these years. I'm not a threat to them."

"Bullshit. They don't want you to be silent. They want you to talk, only in a way that benefits them. They want you on their side."

"They have scores of people like me who live to go with their flow. They don't need any more."

"On the contrary. They're particularly interested in you because you're outside the current. They don't want anyone to be disconnected. You must, in their view, join them and write praise for the Leader."

"So they forced Mr Ha'el into marrying my mother, all because of me?"

"And they'll do even more than that."

I was silent and tried to think. Was it possible Lama was right? And what about my mother? She told me her marriage to Ha'el was in my interest because I would be able to go back to work.

"My mother wants me to write a new novel," I told Lama. "She said she would pay me two thousand dollars if I did."

"When did she tell you this?"

"Today."

"Don't rule out the possibility that Mr Ha'el is behind it. Now they want you to write. The question is, what are you going to write?"

"Why should I believe what you're saying?"

"I beg you to be believe it because I'm afraid for you. They're going to end you, but with silk gloves. Or by intermarriage."

"So what should I do, in your opinion?"

"Wish Ratiba Hanim happiness in marriage and stay far, far away."

"But how? She's my mother. I have to be with her, at least on her wedding night."

She angled her neck and started stroking the back of her head, which was her custom whenever she was thinking about something. Looking her up and down I found her very attractive. Had it not been for the fact that we were discussing a serious matter I might have got up and had my way with her right then and there. I quickly looked up at the ceiling. I didn't want her to catch me—we were discussing my reputation, after all—staring at her crotch. She continued staring right back at me without flinching. She wasn't interested in what I was looking at, saying instead, "All right, we'll go to the wedding together on Wednesday. I want to go with you and find out what their intentions are exactly. I want to be there when they kiss your arse and try to get closer to you."

"My mother's going to jump for joy when she sees you coming."

"I'll buy her something nice."

"But how are we going to act, do you think, the day after the wedding? On the one hand, I don't want to stop seeing my mother, but on the other hand I don't want to hang out with Mr Ha'el either."

"Once you've discovered their true intentions, you can behave however you want. You know better than I do how to deal with Mr Ha'el and his kind. Tell me, how would you react if the situation really was the way I described it?"

"I'd keep on hating them. I'd wait for a better opportunity to break the silence and return to writing."

"I always hoped you would start writing again."

"In times like these, silence is wisdom."

"Silence is wisdom when talk is praise for the Leader," Lama said.

"Talk has many faces, if you like, one for praising the Leader and another for praising the Truth."

"In their perspective, the Leader is the Truth."

"I have a different perspective."

"Well then, tell me, what is the Truth in your perspective?" Lama asked.

The water had dried from both of our bodies and sweat started to glisten as our revitalization reverted into discomfort. Beads of sweat shimmered beneath Lama's lower eyelids and under her nose; her neck was soaked. I reached out my hand and wiped the beads of sweat from under her eyes and nose and then held her and kissed her. I told her "You are the Truth" and "I love you" and "Right now I want us to take the fan and go into the bedroom." She dragged herself over and stuck her body to mine as I pulled her in closer. When I drew back she grabbed my head and forced me to gaze directly into her eyes. I saw that she was crying.

"You're my treasure and I have to protect your sparkle," she whispered.

"Why are you crying? Do you think I'm in danger?"

"I don't know. I'm afraid they're going to steal you away or denounce you. Gold loses its sparkle on an ugly woman's neck or wrists."

"Have you lost faith in me?"

"Of course not, it's just my nature to be nervous. Don't you remember that I discovered my husband was cheating through intuition and dreams?"

"I remember, but it's your husband's nature to cheat."

"He's despicable. He cheated on me with girls of the regime for the sake of his own personal interest. Mr Ha'el is even more despicable. That's why I'm so nervous."

"We'll see what happens."

"Yeah, we'll see. Come on, grab the fan and hop into bed. I'll just go cool off in the shower for a bit and then come join you."

I held her body that was cold from the shower, which I then also stood underneath for a long time as I tried to focus on the love we just made. The Leader's speech was still happening. He made a joke every once in a while so the shouting of the masses would rise up and reach us while we made love. I tried to focus on the lovemaking and to ignore the sound of my silence and the noise of their roar.

I apologize to the reader for this erotic chapter but I want to be precise in my writing. How else would I be able to bear the silence and the roar? The silence that was imposed upon me for years and years has nearly suffocated me. What else do I have to live for but this ardent love binding Lama and me together? Each of us found our equal in the other, the one we can only respond to with love. I would like to remind the reader that when I came out of the interrogation sessions during "Fuck-Gate" I used to immediately hurry back to visit Lama and find her there waiting for me by the only window in her flat. She would open the door for me and we would stand behind it, embracing one another for a long time without getting bored or tired. Then we would go to bed and make love in a way that was unlike anything we had ever done before. We found refuge in our lovemaking, and I can honestly say that we were answering back at them with love. Then we would sit and cool ourselves off with wet towels and make fun of them.

Laughter and sex were our two weapons of survival. In the past writing had been my primary reason to persevere.

But when silence was imposed on me we found that sex was a form of speech, indeed, a form of shouting in the face of the silence. When I had just emerged from the security branch I would be in a state of exhaustion or a condition that was more like an amalgamation of feelings: tiredness plus impudence, anger and emptiness. Therefore, I used to rush to the first taxi I could find, searching my feelings as I wished the driver would just take off instead of waiting for the light at the junction to turn green. I used to wish that Lama's place was closer to the *mukhabarat* branch instead of being located four kilometres away. On more than one occasion she accompanied me to the interrogation. She would wait outside because, as she put it, she could no longer bear to just stay home waiting for me to return. When I finally came out to find her standing in the shadows on the opposite pavement I would grab hold of her and gesture frantically at the first taxi I saw so that we could rush back to her flat. At first she found my hastiness odd and assumed I was running away from something but by the third time she understood the secret: I was in a rush for us to be alone together in bed, so that I could restore my own balance by making love to her.

She also told me about how she used to feel while she was waiting for me to get out of interrogation, how in those times she used to cry and wish for me to come back so she could hold me close until she spoke out loud, calling for me to come at once because she so desperately hungered for me. When we entered the flat we would do exactly the same thing we had done on those occasions when she hadn't come with me. We would stand behind the door, each one tightly and warmly holding the other until the time for hugging had passed, at which point I would lead her or she would lead me to the bedroom. As if time were assaulting us, we would hurriedly and inelegantly get undressed, chucking our clothes in all directions before laying down on the bed to make love urgently and violently, as if we had just been reunited after a long separation, despite the fact that usually we had made love the night before.

When I returned from interrogation our faces would reject any disguise, whether out of modesty or embarrassment. The desire for life and for confrontation refused any disguise, no matter what kind it was. Our bodies would collide as if the two were one person: sheandI.

Our post-interrogation habits differed from those that took place in ordinary times, when I wouldn't dare to try some things or might ask for something new; in these unusual times we would be in such a state of desire that we no longer wanted to keep score. The artificiality that a man imposes upon himself or a woman imposes upon herself for reasons of preserving the impression the other has of him or her breaks down. The woman asks herself, *What will he think of me if I do this or ask him to do that?* In that situation, we got past those questions and kicked the problem of impressions out of bed.

Was it obscenity? Sure, but the obscenity of the innocent that appears without any design or planning, the obscenity that satisfies both parties, although neither one of them would talk about it afterwards. I began to head off for questioning braver and more capable of withstanding it. Throughout the session, I would be calmer and more self-assured, to the point that I even started mocking what was happening, laughing and cracking jokes, making fun of "Fuck-Gate" even as it preoccupied the security services and the Party, concerning even the President of the Writers' Union himself, who proceeded to enlist writer Comrades to attack me and pitch slogans against me, making fun of me or otherwise messing with me. I yearned for my visit to HQ to end so I could go back to Lama afterwards, knowing that we would wash away those frustrations together.

The beautiful thing about Lama is that she respects her body; you might even say she sanctifies it. Ordinarily she wakes up in the morning to begin a precise regimen of self-care. Her flat is only five minutes from the public garden; every morning she puts on special athletic clothes that make her sweat profusely and heads over there to power-walk for a full hour with one of her neighbours. I don't quite know where the added benefit is in making her body sweat like that during her walking exercise when she is already sweating in her flat all the time anyway. Once I asked her that very question and she confirmed that they are two completely different kinds of sweating—sweating in the morning while walking has myriad benefits whereas she continuously cools her body down at home and tries to keep herself from sweating. She also got used to doing Swedish aerobics before coming home and standing in the cold shower. She did a lot of strenuous exercise throughout the day, memorizing a number of exercises and their benefits, all for the benefit of her posture or her stomach or some such thing. Because she has not given birth she still has a shapely and firm body without a hint of sagging or wrinkles.

She used to go swimming once a week year-round. To this day I still accompany her to the swimming pool in the summertime but in the winter she goes to a pool that is for women only and when she comes back she is mellowed out both physically and psychologically. In bed she tells me how when the water touches her skin she longs to be in my arms. Lama's relationship to water is an intimate one and it's hard for me to imagine how she would be without water in which to continuously swim or shower. Many times when I went to see her I would walk in and think she was gone. Then I would step into the bathroom and find her sleeping in the tub. She told me the thing that most attracted her to this little flat and made her buy it was the tub in the bathroom.

Let me tell you a little more about how Lama sanctifies her body. She is so scared of getting sick that she convulses and breaks down into tears when a simple discolouration or rash or even a little insignificant wrinkle appears on her body. She loves her beautiful, elegant and healthy body. One time she complained that her right breast felt abnormal and that she needed to go to the doctor. She was so terrified that she made herself ill from her fear of being ill. I don't know why she was so worried about the existence of a lump in her breast after the doctor had done all the necessary imaging and tests and asked her to give him three days in order to look them over. During those three days she lived an unbearable nightmare, convinced that the results would come back positive. I could never leave her alone during that period since it was possible she would die of anxiety. She was less afraid of death than of disfigurement. Her body is worth more to her than her life. On one occasion she made me swear on everything we hold dear that I would help her to die if she ever got sick with a physically disfiguring illness.

Lama takes pride in her body and knows its worth; she spoils it and pleases it and keeps a close watch on it: it is her spoiled child. One day she told me that her parents used to make her take regular equestrian lessons at one of the clubs where she learnt how to ride horses very well. When she fell off the back of her steed without getting a scratch, she got scared of breaking a rib or an arm even though she refused to give up the club because of her passion for riding. After she saw one of the trainers actually fall and break his leg she stopped riding horses. The flawlessness of Lama's body means that she has no hang-ups about being naked. A woman gets accustomed to hiding most of her body from the people who are closest to her, including her husband, because of some imperfection or the passing years or exhaustion and atrophy. This is what we call the embarrassment of revealing imperfections. Perhaps shyness is the reason why women are afraid to reveal their physical imperfections (some psychologists even base their theories on the notion that women consider their vaginas a permanent imperfection that is something to be ashamed of). But Lama doesn't have a single imperfection on her entire body that she could be afraid of revealing to her lover, so she has no problem being naked in front of him. As soon as Lama gets home she strips off all her clothes and does everything in the nude. She goes into the bathroom to stand in the shower for a few minutes and then comes out sopping wet in order to continue what she had been doing before going back into the bathroom again. In this weather there is no need for clothes, whether I'm over at her place or she's alone; a bikini might suffice when she is alone but never when we are together. She got used to walking around in front of me, moving here and there, without covering her body with a single stitch of cloth. And when she sat down, she would do so freely, without caring what part of her body might be visible. That was Lama: a liberated woman who owns herself without any hang-ups; her lover could have his way with her, however he wished.

CHAPTER FIVE

I HAD A LIGHT LUNCH with Lama before going downstairs. She makes the best falafel sandwiches. I ate two while Lama had just half of one; to help wash it down we split a beer. I told Lama I intended to go visit my sister Samira in order to find out what she thought about our mother getting married and to ask her about some things that were still unclear to me, anything my mother might have confided in her because women speak more freely amongst themselves; they don't keep secrets from each other.

I also told Lama I had to stop by the Party building in order pick up my ID card before going to military security at nine thirty, which is what the head of the patrol that stopped me near my mother's house had asked me to do. I had forgotten all about it because we had been so preoccupied with the matter of my mother's marriage to Mr Ha'el, and she immediately got nervous when I told her I had to pass by both offices and started advising me to stay calm and not to make fun of them or piss them off because they are quick-tempered and might not have much of a sense of humour, because simple sarcasm might turn into a major catastrophe, such as causing me to have to go back and see them throughout the week.

The television set was blaring as I said goodbye to Lama and walked downstairs. It seemed as though the march had finally ended because the broadcasters were discussing, each from his own location, how great the march was, interviewing the masses and directing questions at them about their feelings towards the Leader and the twenty-year anniversary. When I emerged from the building the streets were empty. I headed towards the city centre. After a few hundred metres I noticed that traffic had started moving once again; the scattered clumps of people returning from the march were on the move. Men who had preferred to stay home were tentatively coming out after making certain the event was over but they were a tiny minority relative to those coming from the other direction. Car after car transporting young men who waved pictures and flags and chanted in support of the Leader started to pass by, their horns honking nonstop. Long lines of cars zoomed by, although sometimes they had to slow down and eventually the young men riding inside would start to lose their patience and chant even louder, as their shouts devolved into gibberish.

Two posses of marching young men held up pictures of the Leader and flyers that glorified him and the Party. Their clothes looked dishevelled from sweat and the crowds; their faces and their eyes were as red as beetroot; yet despite the fact that their voices were hoarse they continued repeating chants and praises for the Leader. In a matter of minutes I found myself face to face with thousands of people, mostly young men, some of whom looked dead tired but most of whom were in a state of unnatural agitation, as if the march had not ended and was just getting going. They were becoming more fierce. They took up the entire width of the street, waving pictures and stopping the flow of traffic as the people in cars shouted in protest and continuously honked their horns. At one junction I saw a brawl break out between the two groups of overstimulated young men and some drivers. I heard fists pounding on the cars as their chants were transformed into shouting and cursing. Then both posses were pelted with stones from a third direction even as some people—and I was among them—took shelter in the entrances of buildings out of fear that the stones would rain down on their heads. Regiments from the security forces and armed battalions of militiamen quickly arrived on the scene and proceeded to bash both groups until the young men who were still able to do so ran away and the rows of cars managed to start moving again, although there were certainly cases of drivers getting beaten up.

I came out of the foyer of the building where I had taken shelter and started walking against the flow of traffic until one of the Comrades, who had seized those hooligans and detained them up against the wall, noticed me walking towards the city centre and not the reverse. He let me pass although he watched me for a while. This Comrade could tell I had not been part of the march because of the direction I was walking in. When I turned around to make sure he was not watching me any more, I bumped into the hordes and got thwacked by the end of a sign being carried by an employee who was dressed in a blue work uniform by order of the Party.

I was swimming upstream, bumping into people coming towards me. The longer I walked the more jammed the streets became, and it took greater and greater effort to clear a path through them, until I got so tired that I began to think I never should have left Lama's flat in the first place, that I should have waited until the sun had gone down instead. I continued making my way forward, running into people, and when I reached the junction with a side street that I had assumed would be less crowded, I found it to be just like all the other streets so I gave up on the idea and continued walking straight ahead. It wasn't just the crowds that were bothering me, but the noise as well, which was building to a crescendo with all the car horns and the young men shouting and the megaphones strung along balconies and trees droning with patriotic anthems and military march music and the enthusiastic voices of broadcasters. I had to stop in the entrance to one of the buildings because I simply could not go on any farther. In that moment a large group of young ladies dressed in khaki who were returning from the march were being harassed by some of the overstimulated young men in cars right in front of me. The first car in line, filled with young men, inched its way closer to the young ladies, threatening to run them over. The driver revved the accelerator suggestively, which made the engine produce a terrifying sound, as if the car were about to pounce on the young ladies. I heard shouting here and there. Some of the young ladies were laughing while others were screaming in fright. Just then dozens of men hurried over to surround the young ladies and protect them, forming a perimeter and turning outward to attack the guys in the car. When one of them abruptly socked the driver in the face, all the young men leapt out of the car and a brawl ensued in which the weapons of choice were pictures of the Leader and the wooden posts they were affixed to, as the pictures got scattered and trampled underfoot. While the men and the youths brawled and hurled the handles of those flying pictures, the young ladies had found the perfect opportunity to skedaddle when suddenly we heard the sound of a single gunshot as a number of Party Comrades came charging at the skirmishing horde, brandishing their guns and proceeding to crack skulls with the butts of their pistols in order to break up the melee. Apparently one of the Comrades hit a man who got too big for his boots, standing up to confront the Comrade face to face as the two of them traded insults. The other Comrades stopped what they were doing and came over to repay the man with punches until he was overpowered, at which point they picked him up and ran off with him, moving away in the direction of the Party vehicles.

Here was the moment I was waiting for to slip away as everyone else stood there watching the scene. I started walking but after a few minutes I stumbled over a body I had not noticed because of how crowded it was (others besides me tripped over it as well). When I turned round I discovered it was the body of a veiled woman who had fainted from the crowds and the heat, which had slackened off a little but was still pretty awful. I pulled the woman up and leaned her back against the wall, shouting at everyone around me not to trample her or trip over her. I also started yelling for water but nobody had any.

Another woman came over, bent down and started gently slapping the overwhelmed woman's cheeks in order to wake her up, but to no avail. Three men made a human fence around her in order to protect her from the flood of people, and as I stared up at the higher floors of the building we were in front of, searching for someone who might lower us a bucket of water in order to wash the woman's face, machine-gun fire exploded. The crackle of the shots was very close and we had no idea why the security forces would open fire but this initiated a terrible panic among the people who shoved each other and ran for cover, pushing us along with them. I fell to the ground. The frightened people pushed away everyone who had been standing around this woman with me until some of them even fell down on top of me. The panicky people were kicking me, trampling me underfoot. I tried to get up before the situation got any worse but failed because as soon as I managed to lift myself up they knocked me right down again. If the shoving had not slackened somewhat thanks to the abatement of people's fear, I might never have been able to stand up on my own two feet. I went back to check on the woman and found her in a very dire condition: blood was gushing out in several places on her face, her hands and her legs. I held her under the armpits and lifted her up, slinging her over my right shoulder and walking down the street with her, weaving between the cars and the people, shouting for them to get out of the way. People started responding to my shouts, thank God, and I was able to move faster and faster until some people volunteered to run out in front of me and clear a path.

I knew that woman would die if I left her there but it was impossible to get her to the public hospital in time. One man ran in front of me clearing a path but even when we reached the intersection leading to the public hospital we still had a long way to go. The man encouraged me to keep going and I barely noticed the weight of the woman or the heat bearing down on me. This selfless man was shouting at me to keep running, assuring me we were almost there even though it was still a fair distance away. Without warning I found myself losing strength. It was hard to catch my breath, and my legs started to get weak. Despite all of that, however, I pledged to myself to keep going. If I put her down so that I could rest that woman might have died. Just then I took one false step and tripped over something—perhaps my feet got twisted around one another—and fell down with the woman on top of me. It was a terrifying fall. I drifted horizontally in the air for a second and because of the weight of that woman my head swivelled towards the ground. I clutched her body as she fell down, first on her bum, and then her torso bounced up into the air as her head flew towards the ground. I believed the woman would be killed if her head slammed against the ground with such force, so I threw my left hand out as far as I could and her head came down smack on top of it, painfully smashing into it. It felt like a giant hammer had come crashing down on the palm of my hand, possibly fracturing it.

When the selfless man in front of me turned round and saw us we were already falling. He instinctively reached out his hands to try and catch us even though he was half a metre away. He saw how the woman's head would have been cracked open if it hadn't fallen on my hand. I was writhing in pain as he stopped and ordered people to be careful not to trample on us. Later at the public hospital he told me how astonished people were to see a man and a woman lying on the street at their feet. He found it difficult to keep them away. When it became clear to him that I might have broken my hand, he started begging some people to help us. Three young men volunteered to carry the woman while he shouldered me and we all ran together until, after extreme effort, we finally made it to the hospital.

They determined that the woman had been dead for a little less than an hour but that they would not know the cause of death until an autopsy could be performed, which was not going to be right away because lots of people fall down at marches as a sacrifice to the Leader and nobody would ever suspect that a crime had been committed. Death by suffocation or trampling underfoot at Party and patriotic occasions is an everyday occurrence. Ordinarily it's enough to catalogue the names of the dead and file the list with the relevant authorities so they can be mourned as martyrs later on. They concluded that my middle finger was broken and that my left hand was badly sprained as a result of the woman's head falling on it so forcefully, which left a bruise five centimetres in diameter.

They set my finger and offered me a bag of ice to treat the bruise, telling me that keeping my hand horizontal would lessen the pain. They helped me to avoid using it at all by hanging a sling around my neck; then they asked me to wait in the hallway so they could take down some information about the woman. I found the selfless man who had helped me get there sitting and waiting for me.

I sat down next to him on a chair near where the woman's corpse had been left on a stretcher in front of us, her body covered with a white sheet. When we asked them why she was there, they told us the hospital morgue was full and that other dead bodies had been left in hallways as well. The hospital reeked of corpses that naturally emitted foul odours because of the extreme heat. The man and I sat there in silence, shocked by the news of the death of this woman we had tried to do the impossible in order to save. The hallway was swarming with people who had fallen victim to various accidents during the march. After receiving emergency care they were asked to wait outside so they could be re-examined or so the X-rays of their limbs that had been broken, like mine, could develop. More people arrived every moment while others still waited. As the chairs filled up, people could no longer find seats and were forced to sit on the floor or lean against the wall. It was so crowded that a patient who was bleeding profusely might have got their blood all over and also unwittingly stepped on dead bodies or on the feet of those sitting on the ground. Groups of men would frequently come in carrying someone who had fainted and start a big ruckus while others fell after being shoved by one of the rescuers. Chaos and death, bloodshed and broken bones, the stenches of anaesthetic, disinfectants and putrescence—anyone who witnessed this scene would get dizzy.

As I mentioned, the selfless man and I sat where we were because all the other chairs were occupied. We were silent because of everything we saw, heard and smelt. I asked him what his name was and he said, "Jamil al-Khayyat, also known as Abu Ahmad, at your service."

After I told him my name he stared back at me for a long time. I smiled and asked him what was wrong and he said he had not recognized me but that perhaps his eyes were playing tricks on him. He must have been older than fifty-five and apparently he had been searching for my address for some time in order to tell me his story, which he thought I might want to include in my next book. I did not want to disappoint him by telling him I was not publishing much of anything any more and that I had given up writing, so I gave him my telephone number instead and told him he could call me in a week, that is, once the celebration season had passed, but he proceeded to tell me his story anyway, right there in that unbearable setting.

Abu Ahmad was in charge of photocopying documents at a government department. One day the machine malfunctioned and started leaving large black splotches on the documents so he took it to be repaired and when it came back two weeks later, it worked a little bit better. It still left black splotches but in smaller, more acceptable sizes, especially insofar as his photocopies were considered auxiliary copies for everyday use whereas the original documents were kept safe in file folders. One day last year a Party committee at the department asked him to make ten thousand copies of a picture of the Leader from a colour original in order to plaster the walls completely. Everyone knows the walls at state institutions must be totally covered with images of the Leader even if they are all the same. And they are, for the most part, all the same. He warned them about the photocopier malfunction but he received no formal response from his department head or anyone else. He had to fulfil this assignment or suffer the consequences. Time was short, the celebrations were going to start soon and the walls had to be plastered with pictures.

He made ten thousand copies from the original image. Comrades and security forces came and carted off piles of them, plastering them on the walls overnight. Workers and employees saw the walls covered with pictures when the institution opened its doors the next morning. When he showed up for work the security forces were waiting for him in his cramped little office. They seized him and marched him in for questioning at one of the security branches and he was not released until six months later, during which time he was beaten and tortured beyond what a human being can bear. He was accused of intentionally defacing pictures of the Leader that he had copied with his machine. The pictures were all splotched with black ink. It was his misfortune that those splotches appeared directly over one of the Leader's eyes, making him look like a one-eyed pirate with a patch. He was interrogated by dozens of investigators who made an art out of beating and torturing him, to the point that he lost all the flesh on his feet, his back split open, his testicles shrivelled up after having electrodes applied and they terrorized him by threatening to put him in the German Chair—the chair that, when fitted to someone, folds them in half and is capable of snapping their spine— because they wanted him to confess who his accomplices were, which opposition groups they were affiliated with and who had floated the idea in the first place of disfiguring ten thousand pictures of the Leader in order to make him look like a pirate. They wanted a confession, no matter what it was, so they could close the file and issue a verdict. The crime was obvious to them—having employees show up in the morning to find the walls covered with pictures of the Leader looking like a pirate is a criminal act that is no laughing matter.

In the end, they were persuaded that it was an honest mistake but that nonetheless he bore full responsibility for it even though he worked in a department where nobody was ever responsible for anything. The Comrades, department heads and security agents made things even worse, noting in their reports and the testimonies of witnesses for the case that the man had never been sufficiently loyal or patriotic, that they had once heard him tell a joke about the Party and complain about the price of tomatoes. They sentenced Abu Ahmad to six months in prison, the same period of time he had already spent under interrogation, suffering from further beating and bastinado and electric prods until they let him go, sending him back to work in the same department, only now as a caretaker and under constant supervision and scrutiny.

Suddenly a nurse appeared and asked me to follow her. When Jamil al-Khayyat got up along with me the nurse threw him a look from which he understood that it was time for him to leave. After he told me he would call me sometime soon I shook the selfless man's hand and said goodbye to him. I followed the nurse as she turned people away in a brusque manner, as if she were offended by those unprecedented throngs. We went up the stairs to the middle of the first floor where she rapped on a door and opened it without waiting for a response, inviting me in with a swift flick of her hand. I walked inside and she shut the door behind me.

The room was decorated like an office for the head of the division in the hospital but there was nobody there. I sat down on the chair beside the desk. The bag I was still holding against the bruise had warmed up and the ice had started to melt. I got up and placed it in the waste-paper basket underneath the sink next to the door. The bruise was bluish-wine (a depressing colour if there ever was one). I was pulling my arm out of the sling when a sharp pain forced me to re-sling it once again, and I sat there, trying to remain calm. The door opened and in walked the fifty-ish doctor who had treated me. When I stood up to shake his hand he stopped and courteously extended his hand to me. He did not sit down at his desk but on the chair next to me, opened a file in his hand and pulled a pen out of his coat pocket. As he got ready to write something down, he asked me, "How's the hand?"

"As you can see," I said, showing him the bruise.

He smiled and thanked God it wasn't broken. I nodded and sighed.

"You didn't know you were carrying a dead woman, right?" he asked.

"No. Have you figured out who she is?"

"Because we have so many bodies here she'll have to be sent to be buried at the municipal cemetery unless someone comes to claim her by tomorrow morning."

"She must have a family, a husband, children," I said glumly.

"Naturally," the doctor said. "But there's nothing we can do about it."

I looked into his eyes as he fixed a stare on me as if making a complaint about something. We sat like that for a long time, staring at one another without blinking. He calmly glanced at the door and then got up and moved towards it without making a sound. He drew closer to the door, not in a direct line but from the side, and flung it open. There was nobody there. He looked both ways down the hall, shut the door once again and came back smiling about what he had just done.

"You think somebody's eavesdropping?" I asked him.

"You're a well-known personality and they wouldn't miss the chance to listen in. Listen," he whispered, "I'm about to lose it."

At first I could not understand what he was trying to say.

"And why are you about to lose it, Doctor?"

"Can't you see what's going on? Human beings have absolutely no value whatsoever. Today they brought in more than forty-five bodies, people who were killed by trampling or suffocation in the crowd or errant celebratory gunfire. What do you call that?"

"A tragedy."

"Are you nervous talking to me? I kept you here so we could be alone. I know very well that you're a person who's been beaten down. I want you to know I'm about to lose it."

"Be careful, what happened to me doesn't have to happen to you. You can work in silence, without complaining. Otherwise, they'll come after you, too."

"I know, but I beg you, give me a name for what's going on here."

"A name? Is that all you want from me?"

"I know we can't be fully free in this conversation. I would love to sit with you all day today and talk but I simply don't have the time. Downstairs there are more than three hundred people who are wounded or who got suffocated at the march. In five minutes they'll come or page me. Anyway, I'm sure they're going to write down in their reports how we were alone together in this room."

"You shouldn't have taken the risk, Doctor."

"So I'm begging you, tell me what we should call what's going on here. Naming can satisfy a need, it can shorten a conversation that otherwise might go on for hours. Tell me, I'm begging you!"

I stared into his blazing eyes as they flitted back and forth between the door and me. All he had to do was gasp for air in order to complete the scene. Perhaps this is precisely what would be called Surrealism, I thought. A doctor as old as my mother begging me to name what was going on for him.

"Surrealism, surrealism," I found myself repeating.

He received the word from my lips and then happily leaned back in his chair, stared up at the ceiling and hissed repeatedly, "Surrealism, yes, surrealism. That's it."

"Do you feel better now?"

He straightened up in his chair and proclaimed his happiness, "Yes, I feel much better! Thank you for your valuable assistance. We can't call what's going on here anything else."

He was about to get up and thank me again when there was a knock on the door that stopped him, and the door was opened to reveal that same nurse, "Doctor Raymond, they're waiting for you downstairs."

Concealing the happiness that had overwhelmed him just a moment before, he got up and said, "I'm coming right now."

Then he turned towards me and pointed at the file, putting the pen back in his pocket. "Well then, thank you very much for all this information about that woman, Mr Fathi, sir."

I got up to shake his hand. Squeezing it reassuringly, I left the two of them behind me and walked out, down the stairs to the ground floor with all its stenches of corpses and wounded people.

I took a deep breath as soon as I stepped outside the hospital. The streets had become less crowded and the traffic had returned to normal. But the air was dusty and the street and the pavements were incredibly filthy. The wind blew softly against the leftover pictures and slogans and scraps of newspapers and empty bags of food, sweeping them along and then spinning them upwards as they flew into the air and then came back down to the ground until suddenly the wind would sweep them along once again. The heat had eased up and the breeze was refreshing, even though the ground and the walls were still warm. I inhaled deeply and blew out all the smells of putrescence and disinfectants from the public hospital that had hung suspended in my lungs. I was glad not to be Doctor Raymond, who was afraid of being spied on and of reports, having to hunt for a name for what has been going on just in order to calm himself down.

He wanted to trade that label I had offered him for the many hours he had spent trying to understand what was happening. Now he is submerged in stenches once again even as I set off, free, breathing in the dusty air. But I had first left Lama's flat to deal with other matters! If Doctor Raymond had had to confront them instead of me, he would have worried about finding more than just a name for what was going on.

I looked down at my left wrist and saw that my watch was missing. I must have lost it in the crowd or perhaps it got smashed the moment that woman's head landed on my hand. I asked someone passing by what time it was and he told me six thirty. I decided to go to the Party building to pick up my ID card because the march was over and perhaps the Comrades had made it back to base. I hailed a cab and told him my destination: the Party building.

The radio in the taxi was recounting the events of today's march and every minute or so the broadcaster announced they were going to replay the address the Leader gave on this awesome day. The radio was only broadcasting a meaningless roar, noise in which all sounds get jumbled together, until the voice of the broadcaster emanated from the studio to announce the rebroadcast of the speech every few minutes. I asked the driver to switch off the radio. He wheeled round to me in disbelief. I repeated my request.

"Please turn off the radio."

"You're serious?"

"Yes, turn it off." He said it wouldn't be his responsibility.

"Your responsibility?"

"That's what I said, my responsibility."

He shrugged his shoulders, pursed his lips and switched off the radio. He drove me to the gigantic Party building and parked in a parking lot far away from the guards who were armed to the teeth. I paid him and then asked him to turn the radio back on. He switched it on and I got out. As he drove away my ears caught the voice of the Leader beginning his speech.

CHAPTER SIX

IN ORDER TO GET INSIDE the Party building you have to show your ID card. Several times I told the Comrades at the door that I had come there in order to reclaim my ID card, which the Comrades had taken away from me at the march. Still for some reason not a single one of them was able to grasp the situation. The one sitting inside the door called for another Comrade and I had to explain the problem all over again. But he didn't allow me to enter either, calling instead for an even higher-ranking Comrade who showed up in order to resolve the problem but ended up making it even more complicated. After hearing my problem, instead of letting me in he asked who had allowed me to get as far as I had in the first place. When I asked him what I was supposed to have done, he told me I should have waited far outside the building. Finally they allowed me to enter and I walked through the door into a wide interior lobby that was filled with armed Comrades who were all drinking tea out of small glasses and glued to the TV set hanging on the wall airing a recording of one of the Leader's speeches.

Two Comrades showed me the way to the Comrade who had been assigned to my case. We walked to the end of the lobby and then descended a wide staircase that wound around several times. We passed by many other Comrades who were just like them. The Party building teemed with armed men who occupied every space and stood guard outside every door. I saw speakers installed at every corner, broadcasting the Leader's speech throughout the place, which reeked of cigarette smoke. The fact that most of the Comrades smoked caught my attention; many of them carried a weapon in one hand and held a lit cigarette in the other. As I mentioned they also seemed to like drinking tea out of small glasses. I never fully understood why they loved smoking and tea so much but this was a small matter compared to my discovery of the building and what was going on inside. It was the first time I had ever been inside a Party compound. Passing by I had never thought about what I would see inside or how it would look, mainly because the roads surrounding it were always so crowded with traffic.

When we reached the bottom of the stairs we were at one end of a vast basement corridor that seemed to go on forever. Its walls were plastered with pictures of the Leader and more than one TV set hung from the ceiling with the Leader gazing out of the screen as he gave his speech. A great many Comrades were coming and going in the basement without taking their eyes off the TV screens. I knew we were at least ten metres below street level but the ventilation was good and I was surprised to see more than one Mercedes parked in alcoves branching off from the corridor. How did those cars get down there? There must be a secret entrance that runs beneath the building from one of the surface streets, but how had the existence of such an entrance never occurred to me before? How could I never have seen it? I would venture a guess that one of the car washes, which are typically located underground, must be a secret entrance to the Party building. I noticed some Comrades whispering to one another when they spotted me; they weren't stingy with casting spiteful looks my way. As far as they were concerned I was nothing but an unpatriotic traitor. I wasn't concerned with them or with what they thought of me. No, I was much more preoccupied with that strange world in which I found myself submerged.

At last the two men stopped outside a room, and told me to take a seat on a nearby chair. One of them went inside and the other one stayed there, lighting a cigarette and chatting about me with the guard by the door. I took out my pipe, cleaned it out and filled it with some American tobacco, and then started smoking as I leaned back comfortably in the chair. I was actually enjoying what was going on down in that cavernous basement space. The loud sound booming from the television was the one thing that bothered me but I didn't let it get to me. My day had been exhausting and chaotic enough to shield me against all forms of the roar. The most important lesson I was to learn today was how to ignore noise. I'd like to take a moment to explain this technique so that any readers who are, like me, highly sensitive to loud noises might also benefit. The technique is quite simple. All you have to do is withdraw inside yourself and listen to your own inner voice and forget all about the annoying sounds that constitute the roar. Sitting in that chair down in that basement outside the room where I was about to be seen regarding the matter of my personal ID card, I started taking long drags on my pipe and then exhaling the tobacco smoke as I listened to my own inner voice reverberate inside of me. I would listen to myself as I talked about things that I enjoy in the world or else responded to specific questions I would ask myself: for example, Do I like springtime in this country? After answering yes or no, I would then demonstrate the soundness of my reply with specific evidence. Do I love this country? Yes. Do I love what's happening to me presently in this country? Not so much. And so forth and so on.

Talking to oneself may be a sickness but it can be effective in keeping a person from going insane. When I was a young man I used to love to walk the city streets and talk to myself. I would do the same thing as I lay down in bed at night to wait for the angel of sleep to whisk me away. Once I saw someone else walking aimlessly through the streets who was also talking to himself; then he began scolding, berating himself even, laughing and gesticulating the way he might address someone else. I was afraid of becoming like him so I began to monitor myself more closely. Instead of talking to myself I started coming up with stories and narrating them to myself; if I arrived at my destination without getting to the end of the story, I would keep walking, circling around the school or the house or wherever I was going until the story was finished. Only then would I end my walk. I came to realize how talking to oneself can keep a person insulated from his environment and make him more accepting of the world and all its burdens. And so there I was, talking to myself in the basement in the Party building. At that moment nobody would have been able to guess that I was asking myself whether I love springtime in my country or whether I love the country in general. Alternatively, I might describe what I was seeing to myself. The most beautiful description I could come up with there was of how the Comrades held their weapons. I would say to myself: Look at how this one cradles his rifle, as though it were a little child, or how that one waves it around without fear of it bumping against the wall or anything. There was a crouching Comrade who had laid the rifle on his lap while his hands were busy smoking and drinking tea. Another Comrade made me laugh (in secret, of course) as I very carefully watched how he handled his rifle. He had jammed it in the corner where the floor meets the wall and sat his bum down on the firearm, resting the wooden butt between his thighs, straight up his arsehole to be precise, and because he wasn't very well balanced he started swaying this way and that, as if he were scratching his arse with the butt of the rifle. Look, I said to myself, look, he's getting off on it!

I noticed a small cart sliding along an electric rail coming down the corridor from the same direction we had just come from (that is, from my right) and I thought to myself, What could that be? Are there carts down here too? As it approached and then passed by us I could see that it was carrying large piles of the Leader's picture. The cart continued moving for about fifty metres or so and then veered off towards the right. *Don't miss this chance*, I thought to myself. *Get up and find out what there is behind that turn-off to the right fifty metres away*. I stood up and to make the Comrade looking after me think I just needed to stretch my legs after sitting for so long, slapped my thighs so he could see I was just shaking out the numbness. Uninterested, he let me go as he continued to smoke his cigarette and drink his tea. I walked as far as the turn-off, twisting my torso in an unnatural way, making movements that resembled Swedish callisthenics and slowing down in order to spend as much time as possible glancing down the corridor. The turn-off led to a gigantic storeroom with a large door as wide as the hallway itself. I stared inside and tried to etch what I had seen in my mind's eye. Then I walked several metres ahead before turning back, staring down that way once more. Once I had captured in my mind a picture of the storeroom and what it contained I walked on, coming back to sit down in my chair and light my pipe once again. The Comrade guarding me was satisfied that nothing was awry.

I now managed to sketch a clear picture of the storeroom and its contents in my mind. It was spacious, well lit with fluorescent lights, and had no windows. Workers emptied the payloads from those electric carts, which were then neatly arranged into identical piles on metal shelves; no disorder was permitted. Finally I had discovered where the millions of pictures of the Leader in all shapes and sizes came from. The shelves were overflowing with reams of pictures and every shelf had a template at eye level that was a guide to the heaps behind it. I saw dozens of sizes and poses of the Leader; not only did those pictures vary in size but in terms of the pose and medium. In one area specifically for oversized pictures there was a huge one wrapped up in a cylinder; only the Leader's hair and eyes were visible. Beside it there was another which upon closer examination I could see was actually an oil portrait painted by an artist to look like a photograph. On the opposite wall there were shelves with posters that had slogans and sentences scrawled on them praising the Leader, including one with the slogan that I heard one of the Comrades repeating at the march, "L R, L R, Leader, Leader". There was a special section for storing the large cloth banners on which calligraphers had inscribed slogans praising the Leader and verses of poetry extolling his intelligence, wisdom and bravery.

After sitting on the chair for another short while, I decided to try and discover what other wonders this level contained, including what turned out to be, without exaggeration, a workshop dedicated to producing propaganda for the Leader. I got up and moved closer to the guardian Comrade who was pouring himself a second cup of tea and asked him, pretending I was suffering from back pains from sitting for too long, "Excuse me, am I allowed to know what or whom I'm waiting for?"

"The Comrade in charge isn't here yet," he said, offering me a cup of tea that I refused with a casual flick of my hand. "He'll be here any minute."

"But I don't have time to wait. I'm busy."

"You can go and come back in the morning if you want."

"I can't walk around without my ID."

"Well, you'll just have to wait then, another half hour or so," he said, ending the conversation.

"But I have back problems," I told him. "Sitting for too long makes it worse."

"That's your problem," he said, sipping his tea.

I pulled away from him, trying to restore some limberness to my joints, cracking my neck and my lower back. I walked off in the other direction, towards the stairs we had taken down to the basement. I lit my pipe and took some pleasure in smoking, walking thirty metres and then turning round until I saw my guardian Comrade straight ahead of me. He looked at me askance and then ignored me as a number of Comrades gathered around, lit cigarettes and started talking about something else. Before getting bogged down in having to hear their conversation I turned round and walked away from them again.

After fifty or sixty paces, a nondescript door to my right opened and a young man came out to light a cigarette. Apparently they were forbidden to smoke inside. At that moment, before the door could swing shut automatically, I saw what was going on inside. It was not a small room but a vast chamber filled with computers and lots of young men and young women working at them. As the door closed I continued walking, taking very slow steps. The young man was watching me. I approached him and asked if I could use his lighter, which he handed me with extreme courtesy. I relit my pipe. I wanted to say something but he pre-empted me, with greater politeness than any of the other Comrades had shown me, asking, "Excuse me, but aren't you the writer, Fathi Sheen?"

To encourage him to keep talking, I responded immediately, "That's right, and you are?"

"I work here, my name's Nooh. You don't know me but I know you. I've read some of your work."

"Did you say you work here? Do you mean to say you're not a Comrade?"

"I'm a member of the Revolutionary Youth but I work here. I mean, I'm not a volunteer. I work for a monthly wage."

"In computer programming?"

"No, graphic design."

"What do you design?"

"We design everything. Posters. Pamphlets containing speeches and sayings of the Leader. We touch up pictures of the Leader in order to eliminate imperfections, correcting them and making them more beautiful. Other odd jobs."

I stood so that I could see the guardian Comrade and he could see me, in case he happened to think of me and wonder where I was. He was immersed in conversation with his other Comrades. Pointing towards where I had seen the motorized cart, I asked Nooh, "So you print the posters and the pictures here, right?"

"Yeah, right here. It's the most sophisticated press in the whole country. The computers are connected to the press on an internal network and we do amazing work."

I nodded, and the young man went on, "From this chamber, we upload files of the Leader and his speeches to approximately fifty Internet sites that are specifically about the Leader. We make them," (and he said this in English) "*up to date*."

"Fascinating. You're doing amazing work. But who's in charge of all of this?"

"You mean, who decides which pictures to print? There's a committee that oversees our work. They send us thousands of pictures. We touch them up, crop them and then send them back so they can select the best ones. They might ask for a poster portraying the Leader with a factory or a farm or a mosque or all those things combined in the background."

"But I mean, who comes up with the sayings and the slogans that you put on the posters?"

Pointing towards another room, he said, "There's a special team whose members are specialists in psychology and education. Comrades, intellectuals and poets who work twelve hours a day coming up with slogans or writing poetry for the masses to recite at marches, which are then printed on posters or published in the media and online."

"That is very special work."

"Indeed. It's tremendous educational and emotional labour as well because the matter involves affection, that is, the affection the masses have for the Leader. It's never easy work. There's a room here specifically for focus groups studying the proclivities of the masses, where they invite various segments of the population to come and have slogans and poems recited to them. They figure out which ones are closest to the hearts of the people. Then they have them memorized, and the slogan the people have the most difficulty with is immediately trashed and erased from the list. The best poems and slogans are those that somebody can remember after only hearing it once."

"It's an important consideration in choosing slogans."

"There are slogans that take a long time to prepare. Typically their role is to convince the masses of a specific issue regarding the Leader but it can be difficult to manufacture this in a simple slogan or in a basic verse of poetry. Sometimes they have to stay up late at night in this room, coming up with hundreds of alternative poems and slogans. From there they're sent up to a higher committee that works in the Leader's palace. Almost every proposal gets sent back for editing."

"What are they supposed to do?" I asked.

"Prime the masses to be convinced of certain changes that are about to be implemented. Or to make them demand some change that is going to happen anyway just so that it can appear as though it happened because of popular will."

Nooh put out his cigarette, reached out his hand towards me and said, smiling, "Nice to meet you, Mr Fathi. I'd been hoping to meet you for some time. I've heard for a while now how they've got too much work in this room and are facing many new challenges and that they're thinking about asking you to come work with us. I'm glad to see you here because this must mean you've agreed. I have to get back inside now. See you later."

I was astonished by what he said but shook his hand as he left to go back inside. I wasn't able to say goodbye, though, because I was so shocked by the notion that they wanted me to work with them fabricating the general mood, mobilizing the masses. The horror! Lama had been on to this when I complained to her about Mr Ha'el's plan to marry my mother. She had told me, *They want you to join them, and they won't just let you remain silent. They want to put your mind to work on their issues.* Instinctively I turned around to head back and bumped into my guardian Comrade who had come just then to bring me back.

"The Comrade in charge is back."

I nodded, put my pipe back in my pocket and followed him. He opened the door, allowed me to enter and then shut the door behind me.

There was a cluster of desks inside a medium-sized room, occupied by Comrades who looked alike and were all dressed the same. There was a computer on every desk that the Comrades worked at in silence. They were transferring the announcements from papers to computer. The walls were covered with pictures of the Leader and posters with selections from his speeches. I didn't know which desk was the one for me. Everyone raised their eyes to me, staring without volunteering so much as a hint about which way I was supposed to turn. I stopped in the middle of the room and looked around at them. I had never seen people so socially detached. One of them shouted for me to approach his desk. He barked an order—"Approach!"—without saying please. I sat down on the chair in front of his desk, the seat designated for interviews. I sensed that this Comrade had not just arrived but had kept me waiting this whole time for no reason, or perhaps for one reason in particular—so that I would wait outside—without realizing that I was going to be able to acquire important information about this propaganda mill on my own.

Comrade Rashad's name was printed on a square block attached to the front of his desk. He asked me what I wanted, as if he still did not know, so I told him, "I want my ID card back, the one the Comrades took from me at the march today."

"And why did they take it from you? What did you do?"

"I stepped in to save a young man they had jumped on and started beating."

"Why did this young man concern you at all?"

"He concerned me because they were beating him."

"And since when are you a defendant for those who evade the marches?"

"It's my duty."

He stared at me callously, revealing the extent of the hatred that Comrades of his kind reserve for me. I glanced at the others and saw they were watching us even as they pretended to be working away on their equipment. I turned back towards him as he asked me, "So you were at the march?"

"I don't go out much for marches but I was..."

"So you're a traitor, then?" he interrupted, the expression on his face plainly marking out his hatred for me.

"You can call anyone you want a traitor as long as you're the one holding the pen."

My words provoked him. His face turned all red and he wiggled his bum in his chair. He pulled the keyboard closer and I noticed his hands tremble slightly. I crossed one leg over the other and pulled out my pipe, glad that I could make him turn red.

"Your full name!"

"Why are you pretending you don't know my name? Anyway, I'm Fathi Abd al-Hakim Sheen."

He plunked on the keys and then stopped to read what appeared before him on the screen. He was trying to play some kind of role but he was not a very good actor. He wanted to insinuate that I was a nobody but he proved the very opposite, that he was the unknown one. I took out my lighter, hoping to enrage him even more. I still had the upper hand. I wanted to mess with him even if it meant that I never got my ID card back. He became conscious of the pipe and the lighter, and with the hilarious displeasure of a nursery school teacher, he said, "Smoking is forbidden."

"I know, but as a pipe smoker I've got used to habitually holding the pipe and the lighter. I won't light it."

I nodded at the computer screen that I couldn't see because I was sitting behind it, and asked him, "So, what have you come up with?"

"Your ID card isn't here."

"Where is it then?" I asked, amazed. "I can't just walk around this country without it. Everyone has started asking me about it."

"It's at one of the security services. It seems they want you to pay them a visit."

"What does security have to do with my ID card? They didn't take it from me. One of you took it from me."

"They have it."

He wrote the name and address of the security apparatus on a scrap of paper and dropped it into my hand. I held the paper and saw that in addition to the name and the address he had written a kind remark and drawn a line underneath it: *My apologies, Mr Fathi.* I raised my head to him and saw that he was trying to pretend to get back to work on his computer. I continued staring at him in disbelief but when he turned towards me there was a completely different look on his face. He looked away and started tapping on the keyboard. Writing a response on the other side of the scrap of paper before handing it back to him, I asked, "Do you want me to leave?"

"You can go now."

"But I don't understand. How did my ID card get over there?"

"They wanted it. That's all you need to know."

I had written to ask him if we could meet later that night and he handed back the piece of paper with the following response: *Abu Nuwas restaurant, one o'clock*. I nodded my head and exhaled, then put the paper in my pocket and stood up. I reached out my hand to say goodbye but he ignored me and continued stabbing the keyboard with two fingers. I turned around and walked towards the door, sensing that everyone was watching me while they worked. I walked out into the basement corridor to find the two Comrades who had escorted me there waiting for me. I walked towards the stairs with them trailing behind me.

When I finally left the Party building the streets were nearly empty. The Leader's voice blared from TV screens and from megaphones attached somewhere on the building. There was a warm breeze and the stars were twinkling in the sky as the tree branches swayed lazily. I wished that all the man-made sounds would fall silent, leaving only the soft sounds of nature, like those made by the breeze when it blows through trees with hardy, dusty leaves.

I had become a lover of silence ever since the revolutionaries had started making their addresses and leading their marches. I'm not talking about absolute silence. That's impossible anyway and I'm not asking for it. What I mean instead is the silence that allows for those gentle sounds that are all around us to actually reach our ears. Noise prevents them from doing so; it kills them. Let me explain: there are sounds that are killed by man-made noise, like the cooing of pigeons early in the morning. A pigeon once built its nest above my window, on the stone outcropping that was put there for some architectural reason. In the morning I used to hear its tender cooing but as soon as vehicle noise in the streets got going, the sound would disappear completely. I assumed the bird had flown away in search of food but I was mistaken because I found it huddled in its nest. I concluded that it had still been cooing only I couldn't hear it above all the noise. Or perhaps it had committed itself to silence, like me, because to carry on cooing would be worthless since nobody would be able to hear it. On another occasion Lama brought a turtle home with her, feeding it lettuce and then letting it get lost for several days underneath the furniture. As I mentioned before, Lama's building is distinguished by its tranquillity and stillness. One time when I was somewhere between sleep and wakefulness I heard an intermittent short, soft chirping. It was the silence that allowed the gentle voice of the turtle to reach my ears and me to hear it; I was able to discern it. This is the sense in which I imagined how many beautiful and tender sounds are lost to us because of the noise made by our noble politicians, their vehicles and their ways of exporting the revolution.

Have any of you every heard an owl at night? Every year we used to go somewhere near the coast, an isolated house where orange trees bordered us on three sides while the sea occupied the fourth. I would take pleasure in the stillness there. Stillness doesn't mean the absence of sounds, not at all, but rather the tranquillity that allows one to perceive quiet, soft and distant sounds. In addition to the sound of the waves crashing against the rocks on the distant shore and the crowing of the rooster before dawn in the outlying village, there are other sounds that leave a perpetual yearning for that tranquil place in the soul, including the sound of water babbling in a small brook or the lowing of a cow or a dog barking in a remote village and, last but not least, the hooting of the owl that feels sated after catching a mouse and ravenously devouring it.

The most beautiful sound in the world is the voice of the muezzin making his calls to prayer from the minaret three kilometres away from my building as the city slumbers in a deep sleep, as all modes of transportation stop moving, as the streets are emptied of people and cars, and as the TV stops broadcasting the Leader's speeches.

But the most beautiful thing in the entire universe is the silence that allows us to hear soft and distant sounds.

I walked from the Party building to the military security compound on foot, and with the Leader's voice trailing after me from the speakers strung up on buildings. As I moved away from one speaker, the Leader's voice drifted away from me, but then I moved closer to another one so that not a single word of what he was saying got away from me. In order to escape the roar I retreated into my inner world and started thinking about what Nooh had told me: they want me to work for them in the propaganda workshop located in the basement of the Party building.

CHAPTER SEVEN

T HEY WERE EXPECTING ME at the *mukhabarat* branch. The guard directed me to a small room located near the main entrance to the compound where a man with a frightening moustache asked for my name and then skimmed through a long list until he found it, which allowed me to enter. He pointed inside and ordered me to head up to the second floor of a nearby building. There I found myself in a waiting room large enough to accommodate a great many people but with only ten men and two young ladies sitting on plastic chairs. I said good evening and sat down at the far end, next to a young man about twenty years old. He couldn't decide whether to sit still or get up and walk around as his two powerful lungs pressed air through his nostrils.

The room was incredibly ugly and filthy. The blue paint on the walls was peeling in many places near the ceiling and had turned black along the bottom half from the thousands of hands that had rubbed along it. There were twenty dated pictures of the Leader covering the windows and the walls and a sign warning that smoking was forbidden "on the honour system". I would have taken out my pipe and lit it up but the sign deterred me; I didn't want to be held accountable for any more wrongdoing than I had already been saddled with.

The two young ladies were dressed stylishly, wearing clothes that weren't at all appropriate for the place. What did fit was the extreme anxiety that was visible in their eyes even as they tried to cover it up. Meanwhile, the men in the room expressed their unease more honestly, silently bowing their heads towards the ground or sighing loudly or muttering some things they wished God would grant them: protection and mercy.

A door opened and a security agent with a face that had gone unshaven for several days came in wearing rumpled, grubby civilian clothes. He pointed at a man who sprang up to go with him. The man disappeared behind the door and the agent followed him but turned round before he disappeared, throwing an interrogative glance my way and then shutting the door behind him. I anxiously stood up like the young man beside me had been doing and went outside the room and started slowly pacing, pausing to lean against the wall. A wall clock indicated nine thirty as security personnel moved between rooms, toting files that were all the same shape and colour. I tried casually strolling down the hallway in order to cast a glance through the open doors but a goon I hadn't seen at first because he was lying down on a military bed placed in the hallway sat up and ordered me to turn around. I returned to leaning against the wall outside the waiting room. Just a moment had passed when a nearby door opened and the same man who had been waiting with us and then got called in by the officer came back out once again. I noticed he was all relaxed, smiling, so his problem must have been resolved the way he had hoped it would be. A few minutes later onc of the two young ladies came out holding a cigarette and asked me for a light. After I gave it to her she stood there and started puffing away nervously. I was about to say something when two goons brusquely appeared, intentionally making a lot of noise as they walked through the nearby door, and then came back out again holding another man who had been with us in the waiting room. His face was yellow as they escorted him down the stairs. I turned towards the young woman to see her crush out her cigarette without finishing it. The scene had made her so nervous that she went back inside.

At ten thirty I was the only one left in the waiting room. The same agent had come to summon the others one by one. They must have all then gone out through the other door, either with their fear and anxiety erased or else escorted by agents, as had been the case with that man who was all yellow in the face. From where I sat I could predict the outcome just by the sound the agents made when they called the next person's name. Then the goon opened the door and peered out. He pointed at me to come so I stood up. He waited for me to enter, then followed me and closed the door behind him.

The room was as wide as the waiting room but not quite as long. The furniture was limited to a metal desk with one chair placed behind it and two chairs in front; a window and another door for people to leave through once the meeting was over; a television set that was on with the sound muted (the recording of the Leader's address had ended and they were now airing enthusiastic nationalist songs); two pictures of the Leader on the walls to the right and the left. In a husky voice the goon asked me to have a seat in one of the chairs. After I did he just stood there gawking at me.

The picture of the Leader in front of me seemed strange because I had never seen it before. It showed the Leader driving a Rolls Royce and resting his left arm on the window, gazing straight at the camera and smiling. Maybe he wasn't actually driving the car but just wanted to have his picture taken in that pose; whatever the case, the picture looked completely natural. I stared at it for a long time in order to avoid making eye contact with that goon who did not take his eyes off me the entire time. A bureaucrat aggressively opened the door but turned out, oddly enough, to be a frail little man; his face unmistakably betrayed his peasant background. He wiped his hands on a towel as though he had just washed them. Then he handed the towel to the goon and settled into his seat behind the metal desk. I had stood up after a gesture from the goon. The bureaucrat indicated for me to sit down, which I did even as the goon moved over to stand sentry beside the door.

The bureaucrat opened a desk drawer and took out a thick folder that was the same shape and colour as all the other folders I had seen the goons walking around with in the hallway. He placed it in front of me on the table, opened it and threw me a glance I couldn't decipher. I saw my ID in the folder and the bureaucrat took it out and placed it by its side. So this was my file. The bureaucrat scanned through sections of the reports, all of which were computer printouts. Without raising his eyes towards me, in a measured voice with a distinct rural accent, the bureaucrat said, "You've been warned more than once to shape up. As you know, in this country we punish anyone who doesn't respect himself, anyone who doesn't respect the laws of the country. As long as you continue to disrespect the symbols of the country, we will remain determined to put a stop to it. We have our own methods, which we are quite good at, effective techniques we know the outcome of in advance. You were meant to teach yourself to become a good citizen, but instead... We used to respect you and even liked you for being a talented writer who once had a future ahead of him, but thanks to your lack of respect, your talent and your future are no longer of any concern to us, and therefore..."

I was amazed by the monotony of this bureaucrat's voice, the simplicity of his language. His self-confidence was so incongruous with his small stature that I almost burst out laughing. If those expressions had come out of somebody with a different build they might have been convincing, but coming from this puny excuse for a human being who was so afraid of being alone with me in his office that he needed his lackey to stay behind in order to protect him they seemed funny and failed to intimidate me at all. I smiled, staring right back into his eyes and waiting for the conclusion he had begun with the word "therefore".

"Therefore... what?" I asked.

He raised his eyes towards me, unsure of what to do next because I showed no fear and was not trembling from his implied threat. He stopped flipping through the file and let his arms fall to his sides.

"Therefore what?" he demanded. "You're asking me, therefore what?"

"Just finish what you were going to say, please."

"All right, so you don't care what's going to happen to you, then?"

"All I want to know is what's going to happen to me."

"But, you're not afraid?"

"Why should I be afraid?"

"You must be afraid." Saying that he glanced over at the goon standing by the door, who moved a bit closer to the table. He really was trying to frighten me but I sharply rapped on the table in order to get him to continue and to make him realize that I wasn't afraid. Taking out my pipe and my lighter, I asked him, "Please, tell me, why should I be afraid?"

As he got up from his seat, he gestured to the goon and said, "Anyone sitting where you are should be afraid. No exceptions."

The bureaucrat had turned around to face the window as he lit a cigarette when the goon grabbed me with both hands and violently lifted me up out of the chair, shaking me this way and that in order to intimidate me. He jerked me towards the door and then threw me back at the chair, forcing me to sit down again, but before I even touched the seat he picked me back up again. It went on and on like this for several minutes. My shirt got torn under the left armpit. This poor shirt that had been splotched with blood in the morning now got torn under the armpit in the evening. He pounded on my left hand that was hung in a sling wrapped round my neck, which put me in excruciating pain. I grabbed at him and tried to push him off but the bureaucrat turned around and sat back down so the goon sat me down as well. Forcing myself to look up

142

at the goon, I saw that, strangely, he was panting from the struggle I had put up. My losses were no more than a torn shirt and some pain in my left hand that quickly died down. I knew that the bureaucrat was watching me so I smiled at the goon, mocking him, and then turned back to face the bureaucrat. He was visibly irked when he noticed my smile—this was nothing less than insubordination as far as he was concerned—so he reached under the desk and pushed something, an electrical buzzer I think, and then took a hard drag on his cigarette. He was angry that I had won this round and was still not scared. Only a few seconds passed before another door opened with a roar and the two men I had seen taking the yellowish man away came in. Now there were three goons. The bureaucrat waved for them to take me away and they all started grabbing at me in unison (just try to imagine, dear reader, three people clutching one person at the same time even as his left hand hangs in a sling from around his neck) and dragged me (or possibly carried me) outside. I was unable to get my bearings until they had taken me downstairs. They were squeezing me painfully and savagely barking monosyllabic words. Because I was not putting up much of a fight one of them had to hold my legs under his arm and follow behind the others. As they descended below the ground floor I realized they were taking me to the basement, into custody. A metal door opened and we passed through it into a wide corridor lined with cell doors. A guard had opened one and stood there holding it until they stopped and shoved me inside. The metal door slammed shut with a horrible clang.

I got up and started to shake the dust from my trousers despite the fact that I couldn't see a thing in the pitch-black darkness. I had expected my legs to be in worse shape. Before I re-tucked my shirt into my trousers I had to undo the belt and the buttons; after re-cinching it I tried to make out the walls of the cell but in vain because of the utter blackness. After the goons marched back upstairs, outside the cell the silence was complete and I could no longer hear any voices or thumps or footsteps. I shuddered from a chill, a chill of terror, but the silence was appealing, the darkness quite pleasant and the coldness of the cell was comfortable enough after an entire day in which I had suffered through so much roaring and heat.

This was the first time I had ever been detained. I had not even been reprimanded once during my military service. I measured the length and width of the cell by my steps to calculate that it was three by six steps. Then I sat down against the wall, taking pleasure in the quiet and adjusting the bandage around my wrist. About twenty minutes must have gone by as I tried to figure out whether I was truly happy there or had only deceived myself into believing I was. Arriving at the conclusion that I was really quite comfortable, I laughed out loud because the tranquillity had calmed me down. I didn't regret anything except for the meeting that I would have to miss with Comrade Rashad at Abu Nuwas restaurant. I knew that Lama would find out tomorrow what had happened to me and that my longing for her would only increase, that I would love her even more. After I got out of there we would make up for all the tenderness we had missed. My detention would also make a convincing excuse for my absence from my mother's wedding.

As soon as those estimated twenty minutes had passed, I heard similar sounds to the ones the goons had made as they carried me down to the basement, their curses and their spitting. Then the lock on my cell turned, making a sharp and grating noise as the door flew open once again, and the light from the electric lamp flooded the room. The same three goons returned, hurrying over to grab me and stand me up before taking me back out again as they shouted and swore, bringing me right back upstairs to the bureaucrat's office. When they got me inside they had to carry me because I had stopped exerting any effort. As I said, I was able to laugh at everything that was happening. They sat me down in the chair as the bureaucrat stood by the window smoking a cigarette. Then the two goons left but the assistant stayed behind. I was laughing soundlessly; nothing happened but my trembling from the suppressed laughter increased. When I looked over at the goon standing by the door and saw him threatening me with his eyes and gnashing his teeth, I burst out laughing, very loud this time. The bureaucrat whirled around, surprised to find me wriggling in laughter. He started shouting and threatening me and ramming his fist down hard on the desk. He did not sit back down. He remained standing, red in the face, and yelled, "You're laughing?! Shut up or we'll teach you a lesson! Shut up! If I send you back downstairs you won't ever come out! You think you can fool me into thinking you're not afraid?! You'll feel my wrath. You don't matter

to me, not at all. I don't care how well known you are.
I'm Inspector Nouri!"

I stopped laughing and wiped away the tears of laughter
with my shirtsleeve. As he sat down, crushed out his cigarette
in the ashtray and lit another one, I continued to convulse
from my stifled laughter. Puffing smoke out of his mouth
in a vile manner, he said, "Now you listen and listen good.
You think that if we lock you up the world is going to rise
up on your behalf? That the BBC is going to broadcast it?
Listen up, we don't care if the Americans are scratching
your back, understand?"

This little man had now made several mistakes and given
himself away. He and his methods were now crystal clear
to me. He was trying to intimidate me and he had shown
his muscle with the goons. If he really wanted me locked
up he would have kept me in the cell until tomorrow at the
very least, but what Nooh had told me back at the Party
building about how they wanted me to join them helped
me to understand that everything they were doing to me
was something like an appetizer before serving me the good
stuff. Their biggest mistake was using such a puny man
who tried to seem bigger than he was. All this and more,
especially the comfort I had felt down in the cell, allowed
me, once I had finished wiping away my tears, to stand up,
rest against the table and lean over it, shaping with my lips
that very same word I had directed at Lama's husband and
for which they had dragged me down to the security office
in the first place. I had done all of that before the goon
even noticed or could hurry over to grab me and force me
back down into my seat.

The bureaucrat was shocked. He hadn't expected me to direct such an insulting word at him. He wasn't prepared because he never would have expected me to disrespect him that much. Finding himself in a real predicament, he stood up and said that he was going to teach me a lesson and then left. I adjusted my sitting position, took out my pipe and lit it. I glanced over at the goon and saw that he was still staring at me, as always, but when I asked him to stop looking at me he did.

There were now two possibilities before me: either they would send me back down to the cell, where silence would overwhelm and envelop me, which I hoped for and would have actually made me very happy; or they were going to let me go, I would regain my freedom and be free to seek out tranquillity wherever I wished, which would most definitely be at Lama's. The silence I had found in the cell had liberated me from whatever Inspector Nouri might end up doing with me.

A goon I hadn't seen before calmly opened the door and peered inside. He gestured at Inspector Nouri's assistant and the two of them left without shutting the door behind them completely. I heard them whispering to each other but I could not make out a single word. Then they came back in and the second man approached me while the assistant stayed near the door. The expression on the second Comrade's face had changed and he politely invited me to come with him to see the commanding officer. I got up, intending to follow him, but he asked me to go first, a local custom showing esteem and respect, so I walked outside and then stopped in order to allow him to pass in front of

me and show me the way. We walked up to the top floor
where everything seemed normal. So now they were going
to start offering me carrots. The commanding officer would
tell me he had not realized I was there but that as soon as
he did he had intervened immediately. All because I was
a respected writer and I must have known that they were
respectable people as well.

The goon stopped in front of a door that said "Commanding
Officer", guarded by a large man who opened the door for
us at once and shot me an inscrutable look. Then he shuffled
me in first and followed me. We were in a room attached
to the commanding officer's office, which was furnished
like the living room of a middle-class home. He had me
wait there for a moment in order to inform whoever was
inside that I had arrived, and then he turned round and
ostentatiously gestured for me to enter. I walked through
the open door separating the room from the office, and as
soon as I got inside I froze in surprise. Sitting behind the
desk was Mr Ha'el! The man who wanted to become my
mother's husband. Two other men who appeared to be
high-ranking security officers were sitting there with him.
Mr Ha'el got up and came around from behind the fancy
desk, approaching me with a smile and opening his arms
towards me. The two men also got up as a sign of respect.
To him, of course.

Everything in the office was extravagant. In addition to
the table there was extra furniture—a bookshelf, electronic
equipment, curtains, paint, chandeliers all over the place—
all of it evincing a refined taste and lofty sophistication.
The faces of the three men and their clothes were also

sophisticated and elegant; they were hale, clean-shaven, smelling of expensive cologne; they all wore silk ties. In addition Mr Ha'el had placed a handkerchief in his upper jacket pocket that matched his tie.

He embraced me and planted three kisses on my cheeks. Then he grabbed my hand and started shaking it as he pronounced words of welcome, introducing me to the other two men.

"Fathi, please meet Colonel so-and-so and Lieutenant Colonel such-and-such."

Pleasantries of every kind ensued. Then he invited me to sit down in a comfortable chair near the desk and I was just about to do so when the two men excused themselves, saying that they had to go look after a few things (the matter had been arranged in advance, of course). So we returned immediately to handshakes and exchanged smiles once more, all of us wishing to return some other time so that we could see each other again, and then they left. As soon as we sat down Mr Ha'el began to express how happy he was to finally have the chance to meet me, saying how he had been looking forward to this for a long time, that he had read all of my books and watched my television programme and other things like that. His classiness surpassed my expectations. He wore a gold ring on his right pinky, which was continuously visible as he spoke, his collar was crisply starched and his tie was correctly knotted according to the latest fashion. Everything pointed to distinction and vast self-confidence, except his rural mien distorted the image he was trying so hard to cultivate. In the end his mannerisms were not that important.

He lit a fine cigar with a gold lighter.

"How's your mother, Ratiba Hanim?"

"Very well."

"I called her a little while ago and she told me she had spoken to you."

"Yeah, she told me something about the two of you."

"I hope you approve."

"You want my approval?"

"Naturally, you're her eldest child and only son and having your approval would make me very happy."

He was speaking naturally, as if we were in their family home at that moment and not at the security branch. Honestly, I hated him and found everything that was happening to be completely absurd. I won't pre-empt matters any more by talking about what my thoughts or feelings were in that moment, I'll just record here the conversation that took place between us.

"Mr Ha'el, couldn't you have found a better way for us to meet?"

"I would have preferred for us to meet under better circumstances."

"But it seems like you've arranged things this way for a reason. Tell me the truth, please, what do you want from me other than my mother?"

He smiled because I knew his intentions. He started sucking on his cigar and blowing out smoke in order to buy some time and find a convincing answer. He was expecting me to thank him for saving me from the clutches of Inspector Nouri. How do these people think? I wondered. Why had he decided to humiliate me before our meeting? I think he must have orchestrated things after hearing my name mentioned by the military security patrol that had stopped me when I was leaving my mother's. He must have asked the patrol to inform me to go there and then dispatched the Comrades to send my ID over to the security compound. He came out from behind the desk and stood in front of me.

"What do I want from you other than your mother? I want us to be friends."

"You security types are the weirdest people. We could have met at my mother's house. We could have got to know each other there and you could have offered me your friendship, but you just can't come out of your security universe. You want to lock people up and force your friendship upon them on your terms. I don't even know what your terms are. Tell me, please, what are your terms? What kind of a friendship are you talking about?"

"If you were anybody else uttering those words you would have been locked up for God only knows how long."

"Be that as it may, please answer the question."

"My terms are that you give up your combativeness, because once you're my relative I don't want to get hurt by your actions."

"How could you ever allow yourself to even consider marrying the mother of someone so combative?"

"Because you're going to stop being combative and then they'll come around to you."

"You're sure about that?"

"Yes. You're a good person and you come from a good family."

He sat down on the chair at the desk, facing me and the entrance, and crossed one leg over the other. He had gained weight since leaving the municipality. In our meeting he was no different from any other man of the regime. I noticed he was wearing socks that didn't match, again betraying his rural origins. He noticed that I had discovered this so he put his leg back down and the sock disappeared beneath the desk.

"So now that you've helped me see what will happen if I don't stop being so combative once I become your relative, what now?"

"You're a good writer."

"Let's assume I do what you're asking me to do, and become a good-hearted, exemplary relative. Then what?"

"We'd reward you. Look, I need you."

"What do you mean?"

"I'll make you head of one of the media institutions. Come on. Think about it. Why should you have to be silent when you love being combative, when you could become one of us and get back to writing?"

"Because I'm an intellectual."

"You mean to say the intellectual is combative by nature?"

"You call things other than what they are. I'm not combative. I just don't like what's going on."

"You don't like what's going on? That's ridiculous. What's happening is the law of the land. Join me in the government and you'll learn to like us, to like what's going on in every way. You'll publish your books again and make good money. Enjoy your life, man!"

"You want to buy me off so I can give your actions a facelift."

"The talk of intellectuals."

"So you're forcing me to choose then, between the silence of prison and the noise of the regime."

"If I were you, I'd be more worried about the silence of the grave."

Saying this he tilted his face up towards the ceiling and resumed puffing on his cigar. He remained like that for a moment as I stared back at him without finding anything to say in response. He had pronounced the word *grave* in a particular way that sounded more like a threat. I inferred that the implied silence would be one and the same, whether that was in prison or the grave. I was afraid to utter another word and allow him to see me at all weakened or discover any softness inside me. He stared at me as a calculating smile spread across his face. He cast a threatening glare my way, even as his voice belied a hint of someone revealing a secret, and said, "Listen, Mr Fathi, I'm going to be honest with you, you'd better think long and hard about this. The Leader wants to see you, tonight. At his home to be precise. He doesn't want you to go against the flow or to remain silent any more. He needs you. And when I met your mother Ratiba Hanim I thought it was a good idea to make you my relative. So now I'm inviting you to work with us. As you know, Doctor Q passed away a month ago, leaving behind an opening. Nobody but you can fill it. Your mother and I are going to be married on Wednesday, and the Leader himself is going to be a witness for the marriage contract. You're going to meet him at the wedding party and he's going to invite you to come see him at the palace, where he'll appoint you to Doctor Q's position."

"And if I refuse?"

He abandoned his conspiratorial tone but retained the threatening glare. "Don't do anything rash. You have two options. There isn't a third. The noise of the regime, as you put it, or silence, and you know now what I mean by that!"

"But I live in silence now."

"We're standing on the brink of a new age. Don't forget about your mother."

"Why would you bring her into this?"

With odious wickedness that he hoped would clarify his point, he said, "We love each other, so now she's part of your two choices."

"I don't understand."

"You will. Listen, as I said, either you work with us or it's absolute silence. I can either get married to your mother or I can fuck her. You must know the difference between getting married to your mother and fucking her."

Now I was the one who had to lean back and stare at the ceiling.

Damn!! So that's the play then. My heart pounded violently and I felt suffocated. I needed some fresh air that was unpolluted by his breath. Afraid my eyes would tear up, I shut them tight. I wanted to run away from there, to run away to a calm and quiet place where I could cry. When I opened my eyes I saw that he had got up and was handing me back my ID.

"You'd better go home," he said. "Here's your ID, and here's my card when you are ready to call me with your answer. I want it by tomorrow night."

I took both cards and stood up, immediately turning around to walk out in order to save myself from having to shake his hand again.

CHAPTER EIGHT

I WALKED AWAY from the security services complex because I did not feel like getting in a cab. I had no idea where to go after everything I had just heard from Mr Ha'el. I didn't know what to do with myself. I was so confused I couldn't think straight. My mind was non-functional. There was nothing but emptiness in my head. I was running away from having to think about the two options Mr Ha'el had put in front of me. Each one led to something more terrible than the other. Either. Or. No middle ground. Why wouldn't they just let me live in my own isolation and silence? How did my silence harm them? He told me it was either the roar of the regime or the silence of the grave. The grave is a tranquil and quiet place that ordinarily I would prefer but Mr Ha'el meant something else entirely. He had arranged things in a dastardly manner by involving my mother in his plan.

I found myself outside Samira's building. The light in the living room was still on so I decided to go up even though it was very late, past midnight. I was no longer as excited as I had been about my meeting with that Comrade at Abu Nuwas restaurant now that matters had been revealed to me, now that Mr Ha'el had been totally honest with me.

Samira opened the door after she saw me through the spy hole. She thought it was strange for me to show up at such an hour, especially since I rarely ever visited her.

"Fathi? Has something happened to Mum?" she asked me, clutching her chest in horror and staring at my outstretched hand.

"Relax, I was just passing by your building and saw the living room light still on."

She only let me halfway in.

Calmed more by the expression on my face than anything I said she finally invited me inside, guiding me to the living room. Apparently she had been up late watching a film. She switched it off at once and came over to sit down next to me.

"Where's your husband?" I asked in a hushed voice.

"Sleeping, should I go and wake him up?"

"No, thank God he's asleep. I want to talk to you about Mum and I don't want him to hear."

"What is it?"

"You know she's getting married on Wednesday. That's the day after tomorrow."

She smiled, bending over and starting to straighten up the table in the middle of the room. It would have been wonderful for my mother to get married, if only it hadn't been as carefully arranged as Mr Ha'el told me it was.

"Yeah, I know. Are you against it?"

"She's a free woman. She can do whatever she wants."

I was silent for a moment, unsure of exactly what it was I wanted to say to Samira. She could tell I was hiding something.

156

"But what's the matter?" she asked. "Why do you seem so nervous?"

My mind started to become clearer and I gradually became conscious of the path I would have to take in order to make it through this labyrinth.

"Has she had enough time to think this marriage through properly?"

"Everything's happened so quickly."

"How long have you known about it?"

"Two days. She told me last time I was over there. She was especially concerned about you because she knows how they don't like you and how you don't like them. Then she called me yesterday to tell me this marriage was in your best interests. I asked her why and she told me that Mr Ha'el wants to get to know you better."

I nodded my head as if in agreement but I was actually searching my mind for the right way to explain to her what made me so nervous.

"He doesn't love her," I said. She asked me whom I meant and I said, "Mr Ha'el."

"What kind of an idiot would believe he is in love with her?" she asked. "Not even she's convinced of that. Mr Ha'el needs to marry a suitable woman now that he is an important public personality and has some fame in the government. Mum wants to have a husband now that Dad's gone." Laughing, she added, "She feels like a young woman about to get married for the first time."

I neither laughed nor smiled but I did tell her half the truth.

"He's interested in me, wants me to work for them, for the government, I mean."

Samira laughed and clapped her hands together, mocking me.

"You're a very nice person, Fathi, but so what? So they want to make peace with her and with you. Mr Ha'el will be our stepfather and you'll be like a son to him. Come on, my brother, be realistic."

"So you think I should just go along with them?"

"Why not?"

"Aren't you concerned about my reputation?"

"What reputation? Do you think Mr Ha'el's a pimp or something? He's a man of the regime. Everybody wants to be his friend. What are you so afraid of?"

"The people's respect."

"Who cares about that?"

"They want me to clean up after them."

"So what? If not you, it'll just be someone else. Look at Doctor Q! Didn't the people envy him his position before he died? When he died they organized a funeral for him that was fit for a king, and they put his name on the national library."

"They want me to take his place."

She crossed her hands over her chest anxiously, stood up and kissed me.

"You're crazy. Totally nuts. You were supposed to come over and bring me the good news, not just sit there and tell me about it as if we had inherited a misfortune."

"I'm not an opportunist and I don't care for opportunists."

"Tell me, what is an opportunist, in your opinion? Get real. The world has changed, my brother. Fathi, everybody's trying to get on the good side of the Leader's men. Now, you're silent and hungry. Look at me." She lowered her face and then stared at the entrance to the room. "You have to adapt to the situation as I have. I married the stupidest man in this entire city. I tried to make him smarter but it didn't work. And to live in peace I've behaved as if I'm even stupider than he is, or at least as stupid anyway."

"I'd let down the people who are closest to me."

"You mean Lama? She's as crazy as you are. Besides, isn't it time for you to find a better-looking wife?"

"I love her and she loves me."

"That's great. But if she loves you she has to look out for your best interests. Can I give you my opinion, in a nutshell?"

I nodded, despite the fact that my interest was flagging.

"Do as I have done. Be a dummy among dummies."

"They're not dummies, but I get your point."

"Don't you see what's going on? Everyone goes out into the streets to parade in these ridiculous marches. They shout slogans and they're happy. *If your people have gone mad, your mind can no longer help you.* Come on, it's time for you to get out in those demonstrations and chant for the Leader. Otherwise they're going to stamp on you with their boots."

"I can't take the roar."

"You can go out to the marches and just be silent. You can also put cotton in your ears. Besides, have you heard the latest joke?"

She finished what she had to say with an odd joke, and I smiled out of courtesy. But when I got up to leave she wouldn't let me go before giving me something to eat. We went into the kitchen, where she entertained me with her witty personality. She told me joke after joke to whet my appetite as she warmed up some food and put it on a plate in front of me. We drank tea and she told me the latest stories about her husband. He had recently complained to someone about how he had married a simple woman and how he deserved a more intelligent wife.

We were making a lot of noise and she got up to close the kitchen door so our laughter wouldn't wake up her husband. We drank more tea and laughed at her seemingly endless supply of jokes. Samira took me away from all my worries by making me laugh. Just then the door opened and my brother-in-law peered in, signs of bewilderment on his dim face. I said hello and then hurried to leave. It was very late. He tried to stop me from going but I excused myself and left.

I hopped in a taxi and gave the driver my address. Halfway there I asked him to go to Lama's instead. It was past two-thirty when she opened the door for me. She had been asleep and I felt bad for coming so late but she assured me she had been waiting for me before falling asleep on the couch. I had decided not to tell her about the situation until morning because I was so exhausted and just wanted to hold her and get some rest, but she insisted I tell her exactly what had happened to me, especially what had happened to my hand.

Once we were in bed, ensconced in her warmth and the sweet scent of her skin, as tranquillity settled over the flat and the building and the city, I told her everything, everything that had happened to me that day. As I talked she freed herself from my arm and sat down cross-legged in front of me on the bed. She wanted to watch me as we talked.

"What are you going to do?" she asked.

"I don't know. I'm confused. What do you think? Should I accept Mr Ha'el's proposition or do I refuse? And if I refuse, what's going to happen to my mother? What's going to happen to us?"

I went on to tell her, "I was about to go back to my flat and spend the night there because I'm dead tired but I decided to come here instead, to think out loud."

We were both silent for a long time. I was awaiting her reply even as she waited for me to finish. As the quiet enveloped me I wished we could just remain there, silent until morning, but the silence was exhausting her so she asked me something to which she must already have known the answer.

"What would Doctor Q do?"

"He would convince the people everything is fine. Compose poetry that glorifies the Leader and write heroic novels. He would command the enormous propaganda machine that makes people believe black is white and white is black. He would make the piles of rubbish disappear beneath an imaginary bed of roses."

I saw her eyes growing misty, but instead of telling me what to do she asked, sobbing, "Tell me, I'm begging you, what are you going to do?"

I moved over and held her. I began kissing her eyes and drinking her tears, then whispered, "Here's what I'm going to do."

She clung to me and her sweaty body trembled as she sobbed. I began kissing her madly because love had always been my shelter and hers.

That night I had a strange dream. Security forces had taken Lama and me to a swanky hotel and sequestered us in a room there. Suddenly the wall transformed into a window through which we could see what was going on next door without being seen. My mother came in wearing her wedding gown with a bouquet of roses in her hand, holding Mr Ha'el's arm with her other hand. They looked like they were just getting back from their wedding party. Mr Ha'el stared at me through the window and gestured for me to watch what he was about to do as he started tearing at my mother's clothes, roughly throwing her down on the bed and proceeding to have his way with her. I picked up a chair and was about to smash the glass in order to go in and save her from the claws of that savage beast but Lama grabbed hold of me and stopped me, pointing at my mother.

She was enjoying what was happening to her, moaning with pleasure even. Mr Ha'el got up confusedly and stared down at her, then up at the window. My mother's reaction bothered him. She got out of bed and started begging him to come back, but he coldly shoved her away and moved closer to the window, threatening us with his fist. He was outraged by this disorder, by the failure of his plan. My mother approached him and tried pulling him back towards her, but he pushed her aside a second time and then stormed out of the room, cursing the whole way. My mother followed after him in her tattered clothes, begging for him to return.

In the dream Lama and I started laughing so hard that we collapsed onto the bed.

AFTERWORD

I S IT POSSIBLE for the silence and the roar to co-exist? The answer is most certainly, yes. In countries ruled by people obsessed with supremacy, authoritarians and those who are crazed by power, the ruler or the leader imposes silence upon all those who dare to think outside the prevailing norm. Silence can be the muffling of one's voice or the banning of one's publications, as is the case with Fathi Sheen, the protagonist of this novel. Or it might be the silence of a cell in a political prison or, without trying to unnecessarily frighten anyone, the silence of the grave.

But this silence is also accompanied by an expansive roar, one that renders thought impossible. Thought leads to individualization, which is the most powerful enemy of the dictator. People must not think about the leader and how he runs the country; they must simply adore him, want to die for him in their adoration of him. Therefore, the leader creates a roar all around him, forcing people to celebrate him, to roar.

I had always wanted to explore certain dimensions of dictatorship: the orchestration of such roaring marches and how people are coerced into the streets in order to chant for the leader under the direction of bullhorns. The leader seeking to cover himself with a roaring halo is not a nice thing to see. Naturally he would only ever do that as a means of covering up and suppressing any other sound.

With this roar he also aims to cover up the violent crimes he unleashes against his rivals in the underground dungeons of the security apparatus, those places located far out of sight but which everyone knows about.

I believe that love and peace are the right way to confront tyranny. Thus I wrote this novel about the dictator whose opponents cannot find any other way to stand up to him but through love and laughter. It is with love that the hero of the story acquires the strength to stand up and confront silence; with laughter that he tears off the frightening halo with which the dictator has surrounded himself, and then subsequently dares to confront his minions.

There is another kind of roar that this author never thought the leader would ever be capable of using: the roar of artillery, tanks and fighter jets that have already opened fire on Syrian cities. The leader is levelling cities and using lethal force against his own people in order to hold on to power. We must ask, alongside the characters in this novel: what kind of Surrealism is this?

As I present my novel to the English reader, my heart is agonizingly heavy about what is happening in Syria, my homeland.

NIHAD SIREES
Cairo, August 2012

PUSHKIN PRESS

Pushkin Press was founded in 1997. Having first rediscovered European classics of the twentieth century, Pushkin now publishes novels, essays, memoirs, children's books, and everything from timeless classics to the urgent and contemporary.

Pushkin Paper books, like this one, represent exciting, high-quality writing from around the world. Pushkin publishes widely acclaimed, brilliant authors such as Stefan Zweig, Antoine de Saint-Exupéry, Antal Szerb, Paul Morand and Hermann Hesse, as well as some of the most exciting contemporary and often prize-winning writers, including Pietro Grossi, Héctor Abad, Filippo Bologna and Andrés Neuman.

Pushkin Press publishes the world's best stories, to be read and read again.

*